What People Are Saying

"In the most straightforward and clear language that I've read in quite some time, Marina Antropow Cramer presents in her latest novel a saga that plots the twists and turns that map out the course of families. This brilliant book doesn't turn away from harsh truths but also understands that people are delicate creatures before they become harmed.

–Susan Tepper, author of *What Drives Men* and *The Merrill Diaries*

"Marina Antropow Cramer's novella, AnnaEvaMimiAdam, elegantly evokes the intersecting lives of three generations of women, who each have navigated the world on their own. Grandmother, mother, and daughter carry the burden of their history and regrets with varying degrees of grace, connecting mainly through their united care for the youngest family member—a loving little boy—until illness and loss demand more. Masterfully told from multiple points of view, with gorgeous prose, and tremendous insight, Cramer has created a work of depth and honesty about matriarchal complexity, love, and strength. A gem."

–Roselee Blooston, award-winning author of *Trial by Family* and *Dying in Dubai*

ISBN: 978-1-7327097-9-9
Run Amok Books, 2020
First Edition

RunAmok

ANNA EVA MIMI ADAM

A NOVELLA

MARINA ANTROPOW CRAMER

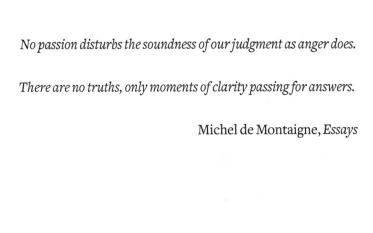

No passion disturbs the soundness of our judgment as anger does.

There are no truths, only moments of clarity passing for answers.

Michel de Montaigne, *Essays*

For Tanya and Michael, with love

MIMI

I don't remember the beating.

Gunther, who believes in the transformative power of therapy, insists I've blocked it out, that I'm defending my fragile psyche against the memory.

"It's in there, Mimi, working its slow poison into everything you do and feel."

"Don't be silly," I say. "I wouldn't even know it had happened if my grandmother hadn't told me. Do you remember being two years old?"

He breaks off a chunk of cranberry muffin. "I remember my cat, Casper. He was gray and white and fluffy. We used to nap together. I loved his warm body, and the mystery of purring. I loved Casper." He pushes the rest of the muffin on the plate toward me. "He died before I was three. Hit by a car."

"You're full of shit. You wouldn't know any of that without prompting from your family." I smear butter on the muffin, scraping out the little institutional packet.

"You're just mad cause you know I'm right."

"If you weren't my friend, I wouldn't even talk to you." I throw the rest of my coffee back like it's a shot of booze. It is cold and bitter. "Gotta go. Kindergarten is out at noon. Come by the store later. I got some green silk in you'll like."

Mimi, that's me. I'm named Anna, like my grandmother, but after the paperwork was done it seems my mother changed her mind. They even had a big fight about it.

"It's her given name," my Granna said. "You can't just change it on a whim, after reading something in a love story."

"Yes, I can. 'Anna' is an old name, it's no good for a child. 'Mimi' is fresh and fun. I like it."

"'Anna' is old? You didn't think so when she was born. You said, 'I'll call her Anna, so she'll be strong like you.'"

"Well. Anyway, she's my child. I'll call her what I want."

At least, that's the way the story came down to me. And I'm cool with it, my name. Either one.

My store, Threads of Joy, is so small, I feel justified in only stocking fabrics I absolutely love. Egyptian cotton. Cashmere from Kashmir. Indian Madras. Tulle, French and Russian. Donegal tweed. Belgian lace. Slubby Dupioni silk; Italian charmeuse that flows through your fingers like brook water on a summer day.

Yeah, it's expensive, and I almost never buy the same thing twice, but the rent is low and the profit margin high, with no waste, so I do all right.

All my fabric is on rolls, displayed in diagonal two-foot cubicles built into the walls, practically right up to the ceiling. I sell eighteen colors of premium silk and cotton thread, and pins, needles, scissors, tape measures. I also feature ribbon in twenty-two colors—silk, of course. You won't find a whiff of polyester or nylon in my shop.

My mother—Eva's her name—minds the shop for me in the mornings, while I get Adam off to school, see suppliers, clean the apartment, do my laundry. We usually have lunch together, behind the cutting table at the back of the store. Then Mom takes Adam to Granna's and goes to her job at the hospital.

That's the short version. It seems to be working out for everybody, for now.

Today, I meet Adam at the schoolyard. We stop to get pizza slices to take back to the shop.

"Pizza. Again," Mom says. "When does this child eat vegetables?"

"We like pizza. Granna can give him a carrot or something, later. Relax."

Mom makes a face, pressing her lips together in silent disapproval. She hates the name I invented for my grandmother, and insists on the conventional 'Grandma' for herself. Too bad. Granna and I like it fine.

The cutting table is clear of everything but scissors and yardstick. "Been busy?" I ask.

"Not a soul. But Magda called, she wants quilting scraps. She'll be in later."

We eat. Adam holds the paper plate on his lap, behind the table. He's a neat child, no spills, no drips. For all her harping, Mom puts her share away with gusto.

After lunch, I watch them walk away, hand in hand. Mom's head is bent forward, listening to her grandson talk. I can't see it, but I know he wears that earnest expression he has when explaining things to adults. For a moment, I try to picture someone hurting this child, then shut that image down. It's not possible.

They turn the corner. Eva and Adam.

Eva

Eva stands in front of the meat counter, wracked with indecision, a pork loin and a roasting chicken side by side in the child seat of her shopping cart. The chicken is cheaper, but the pork loin's on sale. She can get seven, eight meals out of it, easy. A couple of small roasts, some cutlets, maybe a stew. Sandwiches, too. But the cart's already half full and next payday's two weeks away.

If she buys both, she'll have to skip the wine store. Plus, it's too much to carry on the bus, she'll have to take a cab. "What's the point of buying stuff on sale if you have to pay more to get it home?" she mutters.

In the end, she can't choose. She takes both, but decides against the pineapple already in the cart. That's on sale, too, and she knows how much Adam would like it, but it's big and heavy. She's not that kind of grandmother. Self-sacrifice is not her thing. She finds a spot for it in the cereal aisle.

"Hey, lady. Can't you take that back where you got it?" The kid stops pulling corn flake boxes out of a shipping carton, the pricing gun in his hand arrested in midair. He gives her a cold stare. He's got one of those starter mustaches, thin and scraggly, like a misplaced eyebrow.

She fixes her eyes on his store-issue apron. "That's your job, sonny."

●

He reminds her of Joe, a little. Young Joe, full of the self-confidence it would take years of false starts and disappointments to beat down. That's what she had liked about him—the way he came at her, sure that what he had was exactly what she wanted. Well, it was, wasn't it? It was then. The energy, the large bold laugh, the big hands reaching for his newborn daughter and him saying, "Can I hold her? How do I hold her?"

That didn't last. The delight, the hesitant curiosity went out of him after the first sleepless month or so. Mimi cried so much she sucked up all the air in their fourth-floor one-bedroom, all the air and time and chance of happiness. Eva, bleary-eyed and exhausted, would watch her beet-faced infant scream and squirm as if her skin was too tight, her world too tragic, her needs insufferably urgent. "What do you want? What?" she demanded, her own tears mingling with the sweat streaming down her face.

Those gurgling contented babies on TV, and the ones who slept like angels while their mothers strolled in the five-and-dime buying little shirts and socks and maybe—why not?—a new shade of nail polish. How did you get one of those? What had she done wrong?

It only stopped when her mother came, took Mimi from Eva's rigid grasp and held her, crooning in that secret language Eva knew she would never learn, until the crying shuddered down and the baby slept.

Anna had come into the bedroom one time and put Mimi down in her crib. The baby sighed deeply but did not wake. Anna sat down on the edge of the bed. "Eva," she said in a hoarse whisper. "Listen. This child knows nothing. You and Joe, what she sees and hears in these rooms—that's her whole world. She feels what you feel. Now is the time to teach her love, and trust. If you're angry and anxious..."

Eva had turned to face the wall, covered her eyes with her arm. *Shut up, Ma. Leave me alone,* she could have screamed. She'd wanted to shatter her mother's infuriating serenity, to puncture her calm reasonable wisdom with jabs from the ugly reality of her own life. "Let me sleep." She squeezed the words out between clenched teeth, not knowing or caring if Anna heard.

And where was Joe? Out.

Eva could not comprehend how a person could spend so much time away from home and have so little to show for it. He'd dropped out of school two years before they married, drove deliveries, first for pizza, then car parts. He'd worked the line in the nut-packing plant, loaded Wonder Bread trucks. Tried trade school and quit—no patience with classwork, too antsy to learn how to do things one step at a time. He'd ended up working nights at the rug factory, crawling into bed at sunrise, tired enough to sleep through Mimi's endless wailing.

And through all this, the constant motif: *Stick with me, baby. I'll have my own (fill in the blank) pizza place, auto parts shop, deli. You'll see.* Eva had believed him, had wanted to believe. She almost fell for the last, most ambitious plan—a carpet warehouse.

It was his day off. They'd gone back to bed after Anna had taken the baby out to the park. "You mean an actual warehouse, with merchandise and a loading dock and an office? Or just one of those vans you see on the side of the road, rugs draped over the shrubbery, scraps made into cushions and doormats? The guy sipping beer out of a paper bag, looking bored to death?" She'd let her hand slide down his chest. "Where does all this lint come from?" She plucked a bit of fluff out of his bellybutton, held it between two fingers

"Comes with the job. Sometimes it hangs over the looms like a goddam cloud. That tickles," he said, laying his hand over hers. He blew a column of smoke at the ceiling. "But you know, that could be a way to start. The van, I mean. I could..."

She'd had enough then. "Joe, that's just crazy. Those guys don't make a living selling rugs out of a van. They're bums, day workers, drifters, or somebody's retired relatives. They probably deal drugs on the side." She sat up and pulled on a t-shirt. "How can you be so dense? It takes money to start a business. Money. What we don't have. We can't even buy an old car. We live in a godforsaken hole, roaches in every crack, mice in the walls. I can't remember when we've seen a movie or gone out for a fucking ice cream cone. Grow up."

She put her shorts on, felt for her flip-flops under the bed. "Get dressed. It's starting to rain. Mom will be back any minute with the baby."

Joe had turned aside, the cigarette burning down to ash between his fingers. His voice, when it came, was pure cold rage. "You could help. You could get a job."

He never retracted those words, never apologized, but they both knew it was no solution. Her mother worked at the credit union, too young for Social Security, her Roto-Rooter widow's pension barely enough to cover her rent. There was no one else to help with child care.

Eva didn't care to remember the rest, but it crowded in just the same. Joe got a little better for a while, even if the money didn't. For a while, he stayed home more, helped out, washing dishes sometimes or going to the laudromat. Mimi learned to sleep a little, but it was not enough. It was never enough.

She was a cantankerous, unsmiling child, her face set in a mask of perpetual insult, her eyes expressionless while she spat out every mouthful of cereal Eva spooned into her. Eva and Joe had stopped talking. What was the point? When she found the racing form at the bottom of the laundry basket, it was over.

The divorce papers had come through right around Mimi's first birthday.

Eva picks up the pineapple and holds it out to the boy. "Do your job," she says. "Make something of yourself."

ANNA

This is how I remember that day.

We're at the art museum, looking at Impressionist paintings. Mimi stands next to me, her eyes fixed on the Caillebotte I especially like, the one with the woman in the red hat seen through the window. I have a feeling she's not really seeing it.

"Granna, am I adopted?"

I don't answer her right away. Not because I don't know, but because the question stuns me.

I know kids sometimes wonder about such things, when they can't see how they fit, when they're the only one with blue eyes, or suddenly grow, like a cuckoo chick in a nest of doves, taller than every adult in the family. Or it could be a difference in temperament, a child with a sunny outlook in a house of pessimists, (or vice versa), who begins to question her origins.

But Mimi is twelve. She's optimistic, clever, outspoken to a fault. What on earth would give her such an idea? I rest my hand on her shoulder and turn her to face me.

"No, Mimi. Eva, who is my daughter, is your mother, and Joe, her former husband, is your father."

"You're sure?"

"Absolutely without a doubt, child. I was there when you were born." We turn back to the pictures. It's a small exhibit, with none of the most famous originals. The Monets here are mostly haystacks and autumn landscapes. "Why do you ask?"

She walks on ahead, skipping half a dozen miniatures in a themed cluster. "Oh," she says, then presses her lips together and crosses to the other side of the room.

I'm not about to let it go. "Mimi —"

"These are strange." She's looking at the only water lily canvases that made it to the show. Maybe they're early sketches, or somehow inferior to the famous ones. It may be a matter of display space—these are much smaller than the celebrated wall-sized ones.

"Why do you say that?"

"Well, they don't look real. Where are the birds, or the bugs and snakes? The flower edges are blurry, like there's a wind blowing, but the water's not rippled, so it's not that. And the colors are faded out, like they were washed with bleach."

I can see our other conversation will have to wait. That's all right, I need the time to get my wits together. We can talk about the pictures. "Say you're the artist. What would you do differently?"

"Oh, well, if I can't make it look the way it really is, I would have some fun with it. Use the flower shapes, maybe, but with crazy colors—black, yellow, real purple, not that wishy-washy shade. And the water—I don't know. I think I would dump the water, just have these wild shapes kind of floating..." She arcs her hands through the air.

"That's a grand idea," I say. Looking through her eyes, I guess the painting does look washed out, as if seen through steamed glass. "You couldn't call it *Waterlilies* then."

"Huh. I could call it anything I want. I could call it *Mimi's Dream* or *Walk in the Park* or *Number 15*. Anyway, I like pictures with people in them, or animals. Can we go get a snack?"

We take our tray out into the garden, to a round wicker table under the chestnut trees. It's a weekday, mid-afternoon. We're the only ones here, except for the resident cat sleeping on a flat rock in the sun, twitching the tip of its plumed tail.

"This was a cool idea, Granna." Mimi breaks off the corner of her brownie and swallows it whole. "I never knew this old house had pictures in it."

"Not all the time. Now that it's fixed up, the city can use it for special exhibits, give people a reason to come downtown." I pause. "So tell me. What's this about being adopted?" I sip my coffee and wait.

"Oh. Well. I don't know." She twists the end of her ponytail around her fingers. "Why is Mom so mean to me?"

Don't jump ahead, I tell myself. *Get the details.* "What happened?"

She sighs. "I want to cut my hair short, with bangs, like my friend Molly."

"And?"

"And she won't let me. She could've just said no, like she does to everything I want. But she went off like a rocket. She threw everything at me—my grades, my room, the thrift store shoes I hate and never wear, even the plate I broke last Thanksgiving while washing the dishes."

"You know your mother works hard."

"So what? That's not the point. I do my own laundry, and I sweep the kitchen and clean the bathroom. I even cook dinner sometimes, or make her breakfast when she gets home from work. No matter what I do, it's never enough. If I put the dishes away, she'll complain that I didn't water the plants. Would it damage her face to smile once in a while? But she's just mean! Why does she hate me, Granna. Why?"

She drops her head in her hands. It makes my heart hurt to see her thin shoulders shake inside her rainbow t-shirt. Peace, it says, in variegated letters. Love.

"She doesn't hate you," I say. I know how inadequate those words are, but I need time to think of better ones.

"She hates my friends. I can't bring anyone to the apartment, not even Molly, and she's my best friend. But—promise not to tell? Sometimes I get, you know, scared in the evening, while Mom's at work. Then Molly comes over with chocolate chip cookies (*not* granola bars). We turn on all the lights and watch TV, and I cheer up." She flips the ponytail back over her shoulder. "Mom would kill me if she knew. I know I'm not a little kid who can't be left alone, but she never once asked me how I feel about it. Like it really doesn't matter."

I watch a pair of chipmunks chase each other around the base of a tree. Then one takes off across the flower bed into the taller grass beyond, its striped back leaping into view at regular intervals. It makes rapid progress toward the garden's back fence and disappears under the shrubbery.

"Did you see that?" I say. "Here comes the second one." She stares at her plate, picks her brownie apart with her fingers, refusing to be distracted from her gloomy thoughts. "You can always call me, you know, when you feel lonesome."

A little smile plays across her lips and disappears. My offer is clearly not what she wants to hear. *I have to tell her*, I realize. *She needs to know.* "Why won't your mother let you cut your hair?" I stall for time, looking for a suitable opening.

"She says it costs too much, that bangs need trimming all the time. So I found a barber shop that will do it for five dollars, and I saved the money by skipping lunches at school. And Molly says she trims her own bangs, she'll show me how. So you see? She's just being mean, that's all." She pushes the crumbs around on her plate, gathers up a big pinch and eats it. She covers her mouth with her hand, but not before I see her lower lip tremble.

This is not about a haircut. It's my daughter trying to hold on to her quicksilver child, as if to convince herself that in the numbing chaos of her life she has this one aspect firmly in hand. Don't try so hard, Eva, I want to say to her. Breathe. But I know she won't listen. The only thing I can do is help the child.

"Mimi." I take her hand. "Your mother is not mean. She's unhappy —"

"Yeah, well..."

"Let me finish. When your father left, she fell apart. No money, no job, not enough schooling, and no marriage, either. All she had was three dingy rooms that needed cleaning, and a toddler with a mind of her own."

She starts to say something, but I go on. "It's not your fault. Don't even think that for a minute. Children are never responsible for their parents' happiness. I tried to help her, when I wasn't at work. I cooked meals we could share, then watched you while she slept or looked for a job. It was hard for all of us."

A man and a woman come out of the house. I can see steam rising from the cups on their tray. I want not to be having this difficult conversation, not to revisit these stark memories. I want a fresh cup of hot coffee.

Mimi takes her hand from under mine, blows her nose on her napkin. I tell her about Eva's endless disappointment, her pursuit of empty promises of good—or even adequate—income from work she could do at home. What woman ever supported herself by selling magazine subscriptions or stuffing envelopes at her kitchen table?

I don't talk about the men who came and went. There's no need.

I tell her how I decided, one agonizing sleepless night, to stop giving my daughter money. Apply for welfare, I'd said. Food stamps. Get some job training. Stand up.

I look at Mimi, at the sharp angles of her face, her bony elbows, her knowing eyes. I see, in that moment, the young woman she will become: too thin, not quite pretty, with a sardonic outlook and fresh manner that will bring out fierce loyalty in her few friends. I can't tell if there's much happiness in the picture.

She says, "I know all that, Granna. About the jobs and welfare and food stamps. I had to go with her and sit in those disgusting rooms while she waited for her number to be called. It was noisy and hot and smelled like baby throwup. I hated it. I hated her for sitting there like one of those statues in there," she points her chin at the museum behind us. "not moving or talking." She drinks some lemonade, wipes at the beaded moisture down the sides of the bottle. "I'm never going to live like that."

"No, you probably won't." I don't tell her about the money I had started to set aside for her education, from the time she was born—something about which not even Eva (especially not Eva), knows anything. This is the time for another kind of revelation.

Maybe it's a mistake to tell her about the beating. About the room full of terror and rage where, for the span of ten or fifteen horrifying minutes all moderation and reason were suspended, where only blind fury ruled. How I took her, Mimi, away. How Eva stopped speaking to me. How we each drank from our own cup of misery until the pain threatened to destroy any bond we had left.

Some dark instinct tells me she needs to know about it. Or is it me, my need to tell it? In any case, there's no going back.

We sit, silent. The chipmunk comes back, stands on a rock, showing its white belly, its tiny paws hooked in front of its chest. All at once, it's so clear. Anything can happen, in a flash. A hawk, a crow, a cat, a carelessly placed gardener's boot, and that little life is over. Who protects the vulnerable? By what chance, what unfolding of circumstances, do they survive?

Kindness is not an instinctive quality; it must be learned. The thought that somehow, in spite of our best intentions, Leo and I had failed to teach it to our daughter, grieves me. I close my eyes.

When I look again, the chipmunk is gone. At the other table, the woman laughs.

Mimi sits shredding the wrapper from her straw. "Is that why I don't love her? What kind of woman would do that to her child?"

"A desperate woman. A woman who feels cornered, out of patience, out of choices, at the absolute dead end of her life. It only happened once. And you do love her, I know you do."

"Maybe. What happened then? How long did I stay with you?"

"Not long. It was important to get you back together. Your mother is a good person. She was just in a bad place." I pause. "You shied away from her at first, wouldn't eat any food she gave you. For a week or so, I fed you, kept you until you fell asleep, then carried you home every night so you would wake up in your own bed. You grew quiet—you still are, aren't you? And you never cried."

I don't tell her about my time, how the months of silence gnawed at me until my own life became nearly unbearable. Her own ordeal is revelation enough.

Too much, maybe. Mimi sucks up the last of her drink. "Can we go to the gift shop? I think they have a book about the pictures we just saw."

"Of course." *We never need talk about this again.* "Just this, though. Your grandfather once said to me, 'Those who are least lovable are the ones most deserving of our love.' For a long time, I didn't know what he meant. I think maybe now I understand." We stand, gather our dishes onto the tray. "Show me this book, then."

Adam

Granna is my *great*-grandmother. I don't know why people say that. Does it mean your regular grandmother is only okay? That's what I thought when I was little, before kindergarten, cause my Grandma Eva is kind of grumpy and Granna is more, you know, huggy. She doesn't mind if we break the rules, like finish your vegetables or no singing at the table.

But Mommy said no, she's a great-grandmother because she's Grandma Eva's mommy. So now I know.

Grandma Eva is always tired. She works in the hospital all night, has breakfast and a little nap and stays at Mommy's store in the morning, when I'm in school. She doesn't go to bed until after we have lunch. I help clean up from lunch, cause we have to put everything away and wash the dishes, right now, even if we only have a snack. Maybe that's why Grandma Eva is a cleaning lady. She likes things to be cleaned up.

Not at Granna's. Granna likes to have fun. Sometimes we leave our plates on the table for a while and go play a game. Or she says, "Time for another story."

My best book right now is called *Just So Stories*. It's by somebody named Kipling. I can't remember his first name, but it starts with R. Not Richard or Robert, something with Y in it that I never heard before. The stories are about animals that can talk, and tell how they got to be the way they are. They're funny and a little bit unbelievable. I like that.

We read a different story every day. My favorite was "How the Elephant Got His Trunk," about how the crocodile wanted to eat him but only stretched out his nose, and how the python—that's a giant snake—saved him from falling in the river. So now the elephant, who's just a kid like me, can reach the bananas by himself.

That was my favorite until we read the one about the armadillos, and that's even funnier so now it's the one I like best. Armadillos. I like that word. Armadillos. They live in Texas, I think. One day I'll go there just to see one.

Grandma Eva doesn't like books too much. She likes to watch TV, but really she only turns it on and goes to sleep. Bam, just like that. She puts on question shows, where people have to know the answers to get prizes. I don't think I want everybody watching TV to see me make a mistake, even though my teacher, Ms Clark, says it's okay, that's how we learn things. Sometimes the people say all the right answers and they win money. If I won money I would go to Texas to see armadillos, or maybe to Australia for kangaroos. I would take Mommy and Grandma Eva and Granna, if they want to come. That would be terrific. Gunther, too. He's my grownup friend. He makes me laugh.

I would take my Daddy, too, but Mommy says he's far away. So what? Texas is far away, we could all take an airplane. Everybody says he's very busy, and then they talk about something else. But it's okay, I'm pretty happy. Everybody's nice to me, except for a couple of mean kids in school, and they're not my friends.

"Son of a bitch." Eva spits out the porcelain fragment embedded in the sweet, gummy lump into her hand. She throws a malevolent glance at the back of the young woman whose tie-dyed hips sway through the party crowd. She hates her, hates the burnished bare shoulders, the hair in sunbleached disarray, the slender waist, the voice, all charm and innocence, repeating, "Try my homemade toffee? I made it this morning."

What possessed Eva to reach into that precious little basket, seagrass threaded with white and pale pink ribbon, the hand-wrapped confections nestled within the folds of a vintage Irish linen handkerchief? She doesn't know this woman, doesn't know any of the people milling around the garden, admiring beds of exotic flowers and the vine-draped koi pond. She doesn't know, really, why she's here.

Mimi knows these people, is friends with a few of them. It's a trade function—fabric people, importers, suppliers. Mimi had been encouraged to bring a guest. "Bring Gunther," Eva suggested. "He'll fit right in. What do I know about growing organic cotton or making dye out of vegetables and weeds? I'm a hospital cleaning woman. I mop floors."

But Gunther had other plans, and Mimi is home, laid up with strep throat. "You go," she croaked, wincing at the effort of speaking. "Take my car. You'll represent the shop, so they won't forget we're here. And the food will be fabulous."

Well, the food is good. Eva loads her plate with Basmati rice and lentil pilaf, lemony frisé salad, smoky chicken bits on a stick. She adds a generous smear of Camembert, then notices everyone else balancing crystal wine glasses, munching delicately on spears of Persian cucumber filled with Roquefort, quail eggs with caviar. Nibblers. *What the fuck's all this food for?* She thinks. *Decor?*

Her appetite shamed out of her, she sidles through the crowd and slips her plate under an azalea bush, there being no trash cans in evidence. A handful of rosemary-scented crispbread and a Japanese beer will have to hold her until she can get home and make herself a turkey burger. With bacon.

So when that girl offers the candy basket, even though Eva is well aware of the precarious condition of her teeth, knows that wobbly crown she's been ignoring for weeks will cost her, in money she doesn't have and pain she dreads, she takes one. It seems rude not to. She stuffs the parchment paper wrapper in her pocket, and puts the whole thing in her mouth.

The candy is delicious. Eva rolls it around on her tongue, sucking back her saliva to keep from drooling, tasting caramel and vanilla and a hint of salt. She forgets herself, bites down, feels the sticky wad suck the tooth out of her jaw. It's an irretrievable moment, terrible and undeniable, like breaking an arm, speaking in anger, hitting a child. *No*, she tells herself. *Not like that. It's a tooth, it can be fixed without scars. Just damned inconvenient.*

She makes her way into the house, past knots of beautiful people speaking French, Italian, some other language she doesn't recognize, full of long vowels and lisping sibilants. Who are these people? Does Mimi really know them? The capacious kitchen is all chrome and brushed aluminum, a refrigerator big as a walk-in closet, sinks deep enough to drown a dog. Plates and cups—black, white—rest in orderly stacks on oak shelves fronted with rippled glass doors. An army of small appliances, some whose function she can't begin to guess, stands ready to serve at the flick of a finger.

She finds the bathroom almost by accident, opening a door tucked into the far corner of the room, under the stairs. "Powder room, not bathroom" she says. "Really, Eva, mind your manners."

The candy is stuck to her palm. She works it loose under a stream of warm water, kneading the putty-like mass back to expose the tooth. It's in two pieces, the porcelain split along a ragged crack, the metal rim crumpled like a used twist tie. Even she can see it cannot be repaired. "New one will cost a grand," she says to the mirror. "That's a whole lot of overtime."

No one tries to stop her leaving; no one notices. Driving home, she can't keep the tip of her tongue out of the fresh hole in her mouth, going back to it again and again as if expecting it to disappear. Such a waste of time, so much trouble. And for what? For a piece of candy, a moment of sublime self-indulgence. All for trying not to be rude.

Eva steps on the gas and changes lanes, passing a slow-moving car on the right, pulling ahead of the indignant driver with barely enough room to maneuver. "What the hell's wrong with being rude?"

ANNA

Some days, instead of staying home to sweep the kitchen or wash my clothes, I go to the park near Adam's school. It has a duck pond with a little island in the middle where the ducks can rest from swimming. The island is big enough for a pair of Japanese maples, and there's a shed where the birds can shelter in bad weather.

The maples are beautiful. Sometimes I put my book down and just watch their reddish leaves, so neatly proportioned to the trees' diminutive size, their sharply outlined tips stirred by the slightest breeze.

I don't feed the ducks, ever since the man in the tweed cap told me that bread is not good for water birds. "It's not their natural diet," he said. "There's no nutrition in it, for a duck. Bread tends to swell and fill their stomachs, so they eat less of the bugs and vegetable matter they really need to stay healthy." The way he said 'vegetable matter' made me think he was a scientist, or maybe a retired teacher, but I didn't ask.

"They seem to like it, though," I persisted, but put the rest of my crusts away to take back home. I'd make macaroni and cheese for Adam's supper, with crumbs on top. That's part of *our* natural diet.

The man had looked grave. "Who knows the mind of a duck?" He walked on down the gravel path, his little dog trotting beside him on the grassy border.

He has at least two tweed caps, that I've seen. One seems fairly new, loden green and black, with a black button on top; the other is a tan and brown herringbone and has the look of an old favorite, like something you might buy on a trip and wear for years after, remembering that place and the good time you had there.

Like me, he comes here often. We nod but rarely talk, and never share a bench.

Once I thought he was about to start a conversation. I was standing at one end of the walkway that arches over the pond, watching two particularly handsome ducks give each other the eye on the island. He approached from the other end of the bridge and stood nearby for a bit. When he looped the dog's leash around his hand and cleared his throat, putting his other hand up to his cap as if to raise it in greeting, I walked away.

That's one good thing about being old—you can do things that might seem odd or rude, and it's fine, nobody cares. He's probably a nice enough gent, but I don't want to have coffee with him or get to know his habits or see pictures of his grandchildren. I don't even want to know his name.

The truth is, I really dislike little dogs.

My favorite spot, after the duck pond, is the bench near the old apple tree. I wonder how that tree came to be here. Is it the last survivor of an orchard tended long ago by expert hands? Or the legacy of a random seed encased in bird droppings fallen on fertile ground? More likely, it was placed here by a devoted groundskeeper, a man or a woman with a passion for watching things grow, employed by the Parks Department to look after this piece of municipal paradise.

Here's why I think so: it's not one tree, but two.

The apple tree's smooth grayish trunk is split, a foot or so from the ground, into four thick sections, each bearing many branches strong enough to support a great deal of fruit. It's a tall tree, much taller than those I've seen in orchards, where careful pruning keeps the limbs low and the fruit large and sweet. This tree has been free of human interference for some time—years, I would guess. It has grown unfettered, turning its branches to meet the sun, stretching ever higher for the clearest, freshest air.

This is where its cultivated origins are revealed: the graft, near the base of one trunk section, of a completely different variety of apple. The crab apple fills the lower branches of the larger tree with a maze of twigs, studded in season with masses of tiny fruit.

I look at this tree with wonder. I admire its fortitude, the way it survives dry hot summers when no one thinks to bring a bucket of water to relieve its root thirst. I love the way it keeps its dignity, in spite of the rogue branches that stick out at unexpected angles with no care for shape or symmetry.

Sometimes the tree rings with birdsong; sometimes blight or swarms of insects assault it, ravage its leaves, making unripe fruit fall to the ground, hard, knobby, inedible. Eventually, misfortune passes, fresh blossoms appear among new leaves, and apples come.

These apples, green and modestly blushing, some no bigger than a baby's fist, are like the stories in my tattered notebooks—blemished, misshapen. Even those that appear smooth and inviting may conceal, under their glossy skin, the worm of imperfection, the flaw that makes them of no use to anyone. This is my harvest, hidden in plain sight, precious to me yet largely ignored by the passing world.

And that's all right. I never meant to be taken seriously as a writer. Looking at these conjoined trees, I feel a different purpose, as if my reason for living is to protect the vulnerable crab apple growing from the wound in my trunk. The wound like an open mouth, its ashen edges scabbed with roughened scar tissue, a witness to violence that may fade in memory but is never entirely healed.

Sitting here one day, I thought, *I am this tree*. My life, which started out so full of reasonable expectations, when I was tall and slender and full of hope, has had to bend and sway, finding its meaning in adamant survival, its solace in moments of random beauty. Beauty like that small black butterfly with iridescent azure bars on its tremulous wings, resting a moment within the foliage. And it's enough.

Eva. The shock of your excruciating birth, my body reluctant to let you go, as if knowing the trouble that would come of releasing this life into the world. Like these trees, we draw our sustenance from the same soil, drink the same rain, but we will ever be two discordant varieties of being. Your brittle twigs, so easily broken, grope toward the sun in all directions, escaping my protective (or is it stifling?) canopy. You hang your small dusky fruit in clusters out as far as it will go, tempting blue jays and squirrels to strip you of everything you own.

Lately, though, I've started seeing things another way. Are you, in fact, holding me up, at least a little, your essence so mingled with mine that neither of us is whole without the other? Are we doomed to continue in alien isolation no matter how tightly our roots and limbs may mingle? I don't know.

Well, there I go again, letting the metaphor run away with the story. Enough of trees.

My mind seems to take these fanciful flights more and more these days. Whether it's spending more time with books than with people, or an early symptom of some strange form of dementia, I'm not the one to say.

I'm plagued with random thoughts. Some are silly and amusing, but many are of the dark kind, a relentless ache of the heart and mind, full of unanswerable questions. Will I ever understand what impelled you to raise your hand in rage against the child, or where I found the strength to stop you?

He's standing there, cap in hand, the pesky runt sniffing at his shoes. "If you come at dusk," he says, "you can see deer. They come for the apples."

"Go away," I say. I pick up my book and go home.

I'm thin, small-breasted, big feet, no ass. Sometimes, when I feel like taking the trouble, I run some gel through my hair, if only to hear Adam say, "Cool, Mom." Then I spike his, too, unless he's going to my mother's. She'll only make him wash it out.

When I hit Paris seven years ago with my awesome presence, gel and all, I expected to pass unnoticed among the cosmopolitan hordes. Except for a few tight-lipped stares from metro riders, I did. Funny how it was only middle-aged women who disapproved; the ones Granna's age seemed not to care, or even smiled. What is it about middle age that brings out the bitterness in a woman? Last/lost chances, knowing that the water under the bridge is now a stagnant puddle too far downstream to do anybody any good? Maybe that's why some take up gambling or churchgoing. Or both. Or, like Mom, turn their venom on themselves and anyone else within spitting range.

The men, now, they might not have liked my New Wave look, but the message from their eyes was decidedly mixed. It took some getting used to, that naked appraisal, until I started to see the scene as a wilderness video, the bucks eyeing the does, waiting for the signal.

Me, I didn't spend much time thinking about it. I wasn't entirely heedless; I carried a condom. Still do. What's the point of being young if you don't take risks? But I didn't dwell on it.

"Your grandfather had a good insurance policy," Granna told me. "I used some of the money to start a fund for you when you were born." We were having afternoon coffee, the last of my day-old birthday cake on a glass plate between us.

"It's your money, Granna, you should use it. And Mom's always short of cash."

"I have everything I need. I bought this apartment after Leo died, and paid it off with my credit union wages." She gestured around the comfortable rooms she'd lived in since I was small. "I have my widow's pension and Social Security. It's enough."

She'd put the kettle on, measured espresso grounds into the coffee press. "Your mother got her share years ago. She gave it to your father for one of his fool projects. The deli, I think it was. He didn't know the first thing about running a business, thought he could just stand in the doorway and rake in the money. In the end, he walked away from a shop full of equipment, owing six months rent." She'd poured boiling water over the grounds, settled the filter plunger on top. "I told her then there wouldn't be any more. The Bank of Mom was closed. The only other thing I paid for, and gladly, was her divorce."

I couldn't think of anything to say.

"You were such a determined little person. I felt bad for you, Mimi. I still called you Anna, your birth name, then. Eva was impatient, angry all the time, always looking for something to blame for the misery in her life."

"I know. But you've been a rock, Granna. You listened when I talked. You even praised my early half-assed sewing projects."

She smiled, gave her head a shake. "What are your plans? You have your fashion school degree, and some business experience. What's next? No point waiting until I'm dead, if I can help you now." She took out two forks and moved the plate closer. "Here, let's finish this cake."

"This is so decadent," I said, breaking through the marzipan shell to the chocolate ganache concealed like buried treasure underneath, digging into wafer-thin layers separated with rum apricot filling. "Thank you, Granna. Only you could have made this for me."

"So—" She filled our cups and waited.

"I want to open a fabric shop. A really nice one, natural fibers, best imports. I'm no designer, but I know a few. I think I can count on their support, the ones my age who are just starting out."

Granna nodded, sipped her coffee.

"I've already seen the New York showrooms. I feel I should go to Paris, see how it's done there."

My grandmother laid a hand on the folder containing the fund transfer paperwork. "Go to Paris. Your grandfather, who would have loved you with all his heart, approves."

"Come with me, Granna! Let's have a grand adventure."

"No, Mimi. For me, sneaking a bite of this sinful cake, drinking forbidden coffee, is all the adventure I need. This is your journey. Go."

I went. I spent hours watching, listening, talking, thinking. Walking. I learned the art of lingering in French cafés. They're pretty much all the same, with the same continental socialist chic that morphs self-indulgence into necessity, served with a hearty dose of Gallic *insouciance*. Coffee, pastry, cheese, wine, beer. OK, my favorite haunt, La Bonne Chance, did make a superior *croque-monsieur*, if you happened to be in the mood for a grilled ham and cheese sandwich. I'll give you that.

On Paris streets, as much as in the shops and showrooms, I saw the difference between trendiness and style. I decoded the meaning of elegance, understood the elemental function of the cut, the drape, the cloth.

I didn't have to go to Paris to learn these lessons. There was no secret to discover that I couldn't have picked up in New York. But there was something. Granna had been right, maybe without quite knowing it herself. I saw the contradictions that had so intrigued my grandfather, whether in history, or buildings, or food. I recognized the irresistible inclination to go a little too far.

The French had the glory of Napoleon and the shame of Nazi collaboration. They had embraced, or at least allowed for, rococo architecture and I. M. Pei, the spirit of free love buttressed by the saints and martyrs of Notre Dame. At La Bonne Chance, the *croque-monsieur* was smothered in totally superfluous béchamel sauce you simply couldn't do without.

I was ready for Paris. Was I also ready for Étienne?

"Bordeaux blanc." The voice over my shoulder was young, male, a trifle on the high side.

I was on line at La Bonne Chance, trying to convince the woman at the counter I really wanted *café au lait* in a bowl at three-thirty in the afternoon. She had plunked it down in front of me and collected my money, dripping disdain from her fingertips.

She was already reaching for a wine glass to serve the next customer. I heard foot-shuffling and throat-clearing, annoyed murmuring behind me. I didn't care. When it comes to attitude, I've always had more than enough.

There were two empty tables. One was in the far back corner, next to a staircase leading to a storage loft. The other was next to a distracted young woman with a whiny little dog on a leash and a crying baby. The man and I were exactly the same height, though he had a few pounds on me. We stood eye to eye a moment. He nodded. I smiled. We moved toward the back.

"Do you mind?" he asked in English.

I shook my head, smiled again. He sipped his wine. I lifted the coffee bowl with both hands and sucked off the milk foam, trying not to slurp.

"You are American, yes?"

"It must be obvious."

"*Oui.* In France, we drink *café au lait* like that only at breakfast. Or maybe to give your grandmother at bedtime, with yesterday's *baguette*." The way he said *in France*, using that everybody-knows-this-but-you tone, I knew I would be ordering *café au lait*, in a bowl, anytime I damn well felt like it.

"Not *my* grandmother," I snapped.

He laughed, a big, phony stage laugh, head back, hands up. He drained his wine and went to get another, came back with a chocolate bar. The dark kind, with hazelnuts.

"Étienne," he said. He broke the chocolate into segments and laid it on the table between us.

"Mimi," I replied, after a suitable pause.

"Ah, *La Bohème*," he intoned, as if my having the name of a doomed character from a sentimental Italian opera set in nineteenth-century Paris explained everything.

Maybe it was the chocolate. We started to talk. Between my phrasebook French and his high-school English, it worked well enough, though I didn't have the words to describe my business plans. It didn't matter. Parisians assumed everyone who could, would, sooner or later, come and be charmed. But of course. You didn't need a reason to be here.

He was a couple of years out of art school, dabbled in theater, wrote the occasional poem, supported himself with freelance editing. He was, what's the word? A dilettante.

"You like correcting the work of others," I said. It was not a question.

He shrugged. "I have," he flicked two fingers of one hand at his temple, "an ear."

I have two of them, I thought.

I must have said it out loud, because he laughed again, then grew serious, held out his hand. "Let's walk, Mimi."

We'd be in bed together by day's end, and we both knew it.

EVA

The dentist's office is a surprise—she had expected a window-less waiting room with plastic chairs, motel art on colorless wall-paper, and one, maybe two examining rooms filled with outdated equipment. Torture chambers. The dentist would be fiftyish, she'd imagined, bald, glasses, a few extra pounds.

The place is huge. Velvety seating, with water lilies, sunflowers, other Impressionist prints she can't name hung at tasteful inter-vals on blue-gray walls. A counter some thirty feet long, staffed by a fleet of pastel-gowned assistants, stretches across the far end of the room.

"Holy cow," Eva mumbles. "This'll cost a bundle. And me with no insurance."

The girls bustle around behind the counter, answering tele-phones, shuttling between filing cabinets and computer termi-nals. They are all so young; they chatter about boyfriends, shopping, going out. Life is fun. *They must retire at twenty-two*, Eva thinks, not without envy. *Not a single wrinkle among them.*

Leafing through a magazine, she glances at photographs of models with tousled hair and tight pants, their shirts unbuttoned to reveal voluptuous flesh. *And that's only the men.* She winces at her own joke and turns to the picture window, suddenly nervous.

It's been raining all morning. Sparrows bathe in fresh puddles, with much flapping of wings and ecstatic twittering. Are their lives really so simple, their existence made complete by a casually dis-carded crust of bread, a bird feeder kept provisioned by the mag-nanimity of an unseen hand? What is it like to live untroubled by memories of yesterday's battles?

"Eva? This way, please." Her reverie interrupted, she follows the adolescent attendant down a long corridor painted rosy peach and adorned with modern, bright-colored oils. Rooms of mint green, crystal blue, light yellow, some of them no bigger than an office cubicle, each displaying a different graphic or painting, float past.

This place is a factory, she thinks, catching glimpses of acquiescent patients undergoing stages of unpronounceable procedures. *A goddam factory*. Ghostly hospital-gowned figures are everywhere, performing mysterious tasks with space-age equipment.

People with fixed smiles and plastic name tags guide her from room to room—Laurie for x-rays, Sharon for medical history, Mr. Reiss for financial arrangements.

"We'd like to have the bill paid by the time the work is completed," he says, smiling.

"I'd like nothing better myself," she replies. *But don't bet on it.*

Insipid easy-listening music follows her everywhere, permeating the doorless rooms and spaces, crowding into her head no matter how hard she tries to block it out. All violins and cocktail-lounge pianos; no chance in hell of a snatch of Janis Joplin or maybe a bit of Dylan.

At long last, they seat her in a comfortable tweed-and-vinyl chair, fasten a paper bib around her neck, and promise, "The doctor will be right in."

Eva sinks into the seat, feeling fidgety; the theme from *A Summer Place* thrums on her nerves. Is it too late to run? What's so bad about living without a tooth? But no, the hole is near the front, in her lower jaw; it would show when she smiles. *What's there to smile about, anyway?* Adam, she reminds herself. There's Adam. He loves her. But she knows her grandson wouldn't care about a missing tooth, though he would certainly notice.

The assistant comes in, fills a six-inch hypodermic from a sealed vial, and lays it on the tray. Eva's face drains of all color. She stiffens, grips the arms of the chair; her knuckles go white. "Oh, God," she wails. "Not that."

The dentist is young, blond, not handsome, exactly, but appealing. He appraises her with sympathetic eyes. "Did they tell you not to eat breakfast? Good. I've scheduled you for an hour and forty-five minutes, so we can get most of the work done today."

He picks up the hypodermic, sees her flinch and try to disappear into the depths of the chair. He puts the needle down. "Listen, Eva." He checks her file. "You're not allergic to nitrous oxide, laughing gas? Let's start with that, it will help you relax."

The assistant—Shirley, according to her name tag—administers the gas while he stands by with the novocaine. He plunges the needle into her gums, balancing a drop of the drug on the tip so she never feels the prick. He turns away, speaking softly in dental jargon to Shirley, collecting instruments and paraphernalia on the little blue tray.

Eva feels the gas relax her; there's a faint buzzing in her ears, an oddly pleasant floating sensation. Her arms and legs seem remote, detached from her body but not quite out of her control. She is aware of movement around her, but has lost all interest, all inhibition. They can do what they like with her, she doesn't mind. That song on the Muzak loop, it sounds familiar, she knows all the words, what is it called? Something about love, heartbreak. *Whatever.*

"How does it feel now?" He's bending over her, his face inches from hers. There is the crinkle of a smile around his eyes. She notes the texture of his skin, fine and fair and smooth. *No stubble*, she thinks, resisting the urge to touch. "Is it numb?"

She nods. *It's been numb for years, doctor.*

The dentist goes to work. Open. Close. Lift your chin a bit. That's it. A little wider, please. You're doing great. Close. Bite down.

Eva closes her eyes and lets her mind wander. Faces, places, snatches of conversation she had long forgotten surface like a dream, blending with surreal distorted images that shift, overlap, and fade out like scenes from a bad movie.

It's summer, she's lying on the beach. There's another body very close, she can see beads of sweat in the small of his back, grains of sand stuck to his shoulder blades. They talk a little, words full of double meanings. It's intolerably hot. He runs one maddening finger slowly along the edges of her swim suit. She shivers. Is it Joe? Does it matter?

Another time, or is it the same day? A small table in a sunlit room, flowers. Icy drinks in tall glasses etched with citrus slices—limes, oranges, lemons. It *is* Joe. They banter, laugh, pass a damp joint from hand to hand. The words turn into bitter poisoned barbs that hit their mark with a deadly malice from which no return is possible. Their faces, distorted by cruelty, lock in combat. Relentless sunshine bathes everything in a hollow warmth that obliterates every vestige of tenderness and leaves nothing in its place.

Let me out of here, Eva tries to shout, but the many fingers in her mouth reduce the sound to a gurgle. "You OK?" a woman's voice asks, her face safe behind its surgical mask. "Try not to move your head. We're almost done." Eva hears the hum of the vacuum pump suctioning debris from her tongue, but feels nothing.

And here's the child, big eyes clouded with panic, the little pointed chin quivering, pink panties in a soggy heap at her bare feet. A hand—*my hand? No, it can't be*—arrested in midair.

Eva moans. "Are you in pain?" the woman's voice is at her ear, solicitous. *No. Probably. I don't know. Yes.* Eva shakes her head. "OK, honey, just a few minutes more."

There are no more visions, just a great swirling blank space, a medley of Beatles songs made commonplace by a banal instrumental arrangement. Eva sinks into the void; she may have slept a little, can't be sure.

She feels the doctor's fingers brush against her lip, sending a slow electric spasm up her spine. His serious, preoccupied face drifts in and out of her field of vision. When he notices her watching, he smiles.

"I had to remove the post," he says, "and put in a new one. Now I'll take an impression for your crown, and we'll be done for today." His voice is deep for a man so young, and so melodious she would not have been surprised to hear him burst into song.

His hands flash by her face. How finely formed they are, how elegant the fingers with their manicured nails. What would it be like to have hands like that cup her face, stroke her hair, caress her shoulders and breasts? He reaches in front of her to take something from the assistant. Eva admires his arm, brushed with fine golden hair, the muscles rippling slightly when he moves. She closes her eyes, overcome by desire.

"Bite down on this, please." His hand is on her jaw, each finger burning an impression into her skin. "And hold."

Eva sits with the gummy, chalky substance pressed between her teeth. She grunts through the obstruction in her mouth, nods. She hears his voice, his laughter, somewhere behind her in the hall. The music is haunting now, something Classical Lite, one of those tunes you feel you've always known. Her head spins. She wonders how he might wake her if she fell asleep. Would he lean close and say her name? Would he touch?

The dentist removes the mold from her mouth and is gone. Shirley wipes saliva and bits of clay from Eva's chin. Slowly, as the assistant returns the chair to its upright position, the tears come. Eva weeps silently; the tears stream down her face, soaking her sweater. It's as if the forbidden reservoir where she had stored away all her mistakes and disappointments has been opened, as if she's been waiting years for someone, no matter who, to touch her face with gentle hands, no matter for what reason.

"It's all right," the assistant croons, handing her a box of tissues. "It's the gas. It happens sometimes, if you're tense."

Adam

At Grandma Eva's we watch videos. *Bambi*, *Pinocchio*, *Snow White*. That one has some scary parts, like when she's running away from the man with the knife, and the trees make faces and try to grab her. And the queen drinks that bad drink and turns into a witch, and hurts Snow White. And then there's kissing. But the dwarfs are funny.

My favorite video is *Charlotte's Web*, because of all the animals. Especially that rat who eats all the garbage. Yuchh. It's kind of sad that the baby spiders never know their mommy, but I guess for spiders it's okay. I wonder where their daddy is, if he's far away, like mine.

I don't know why Grandma Eva gets so mad. I like staying with Granna. She lives upstairs from Grandma Eva, on the third floor. Grandma Eva's apartment is on the first floor. When it's time for her to go to sleep before her hospital job, she stands at the bottom of the stairs and watches me run up to Granna's. When I get to the top, Granna calls down, "Okay, Eva," and everybody closes the door. I'm a package for speedy delivery, waiting for Mommy to come get me when she's done working.

After I get there, we take naps. Well, Granna does. I look at a book or draw pictures. Granna snores, just like they do in cartoons. Grandma Eva doesn't let me watch cartoons; she says there's too much blowing things up, and hitting. Maybe she doesn't know it's not real.

Later, if Granna is not too tired, we walk to the park to feed the ducks. We used to give them old bread, but Granna says it makes them sick, so now we bring sunflower seeds or carrot peels. I guess the other people don't know about that, they mostly bring bread, and the ducks don't care, they eat everything. Quack.

If it's raining, but not too hard, I put on my slicker and Granna takes her black umbrella and we go anyway. The ducks are always happy to see us. I like the way they come out of the pond and walk right up to the fence to get their treats. They shake their feathers and *waddle* on their funny feet, and they quack quack quack like they're laughing. Granna says that's what it's called when they walk like that, rolling from side to side. *Waddle.*

When Granna's having a tired day, we stay home. We read stories or play a game until it's time to make supper. "Can I help you, Granna?" I always say.

Sometimes yes, sometimes no. No thank you. Then I bring my writing pad into the kitchen and practice my letters while Granna cooks. Most days, Mommy has supper with us, and sometimes Gunther, too. If Gunther comes, it's like a birthday party, only no cake.

Anna

The way I feel today, I wouldn't mind staying home, but Adam is excited for story hour at the library. There's an author coming to talk about her books. He's never met an author, and I don't want to disappoint him. Maybe another cup of coffee will help dispel this weariness.

I can almost see Eva's disapproving face when I fill my cup, can almost hear her saying, "That stuff's poison for you, Ma. At least put some milk in it."

As if I don't know it.

The cup feels good in my hands, warming away the ache in my fingers. When did that start? I don't mind being old, having so many things to look back on, most of them good. Even the bad ones—well, what happened, happened. We tried to make the best of it, didn't we.

What I could do without is these reminders of frailty, some Great Disciplinarian telling me to act my age. No need to shake that finger at me. I know better than anyone how old I am.

My left knee announces a change in the weather faster than any barometer. And what's with this heart? The way it rattles around sometimes takes my breath away. But nobody needs to know. I take my pills, close my eyes until it passes. Adam is the only one who notices. Adam notices everything.

The coffee restores me; I knew it would. I finish it just as Adam is racing up the stairs from Eva's apartment, his feet hammering with young energy. "Is it time for the library, Granna?" His face is glowing. "Let's go!"

I can't let him down.

The author is forty-ish, curly-haired, cheerful. She's written a series of animal adventure stories, not unlike *Wind in the Willows*, only with some evil thrown in, and magic to help defeat it. She sits in an upholstered chair, the children in a semicircle on the floor. Adam is right in the middle, in the front row.

"Is there an armadillo?" he wants to know before the author has said so much as 'hello'. His face is eager and also serious.

I see her suppress a smile. I give her credit for knowing when not to laugh at a child's question. "Not yet," she says. "But there might be, if a story takes place in South America or the American southwest."

"Texas," Adam says.

She nods, goes on to describe one of the tales she's dreamed up. The excerpt she reads is full of action and lively dialogue. Rabbits and foxes. It's a new take on the familiar riddle: how to cross the river together without getting eaten. Fox runs a ferry service, rabbit needs to get to the other side to see his grandpa. The story is full of dangers and includes a gentle lesson on the unexpected drawbacks of being invisible.

The children listen with only minimal fidgeting. They laugh at the funny parts.

"What would you do, if you were the rabbit, to get across?" The author scans her audience. "Would you talk to the fox? What would you say?"

"I would call my daddy," somebody says.

A little girl in sparkly rainbow sneakers brings her fist down on her knee. "Bop the fox on the head," she says.

Adam looks thoughtful. "Foxes eat rabbits. It's dumb to talk to them. I would run and hide, wait for the fox to take a nap. Or I would get my rabbit buddies to run around, zip zip zip, so the fox gets confused. There are lots of rabbits, everybody knows that. Then I would hop on the raft and go see my grandpa." He takes a breath. "Without being invisible," he adds. "Just smart."

He's seen through the gimmick. Good for him.

The kids get up and wander around, shepherded by their grannies and nannies. I approach the author. "Why did you choose rabbits? Because they're vulnerable, like kids?"

"Good question," she says. I hate when people say that. It often means they don't have a good answer. "Rabbits live just about everywhere on earth. Rabbits and mice. And we already have many mouse books, don't we. So I can vary the settings, get in some geography and natural history, while showing how they solve problems and escape danger. How they think they need magic but discover they can use their own ingenuity to stay alive."

I'm not a great writer, but that seems like a thin premise to me. "How many several ways hath death to surprise us," I mutter.

"Pardon?"

"Montaigne," I say, then smile to soften what probably sounded like an insult. "I'm sure kids like your stories. Thank you for coming to talk to them."

Adam is waiting for me at the circulation desk, a picture book tucked under his arm. "Do you want the rabbit book? If we buy it the author will sign it for you," I offer. It seems only fair.

"No, Granna. I want to borrow this one. It has armadillos."

Eva

Eva stares at the contents of her refrigerator. Whole wheat bread. Plain yogurt. A cucumber, half an onion, some kale starting to gray around the edges. In the freezer, a pair of chicken thighs, a jar of carrot/potato soup at least a month old, bargain-brand ice milk, a pound of ground turkey, a piece of fish of indeterminate variety.

Yeah, she could eat. She wouldn't starve. There was even a beer, up in the cabinet above the sink, behind the granola.

"Fuck it," she says. She slams the fridge shut and reaches for her handbag. She doesn't have to look inside, she knows Betty's twenty is in there, burning a hole in her wallet. She'll go down to Elsie's Hut, why not? It's been four, six months since the last time she went out, easy.

Besides, the beer at home is warm. "Tastes like dishwater," Eva says. She can just hear Mimi say, in that icy voice, "How do you know what dishwater tastes like?" Mimi's so smart she has an answer for everything.

Mimi. Everybody thinks I changed her name because I read it in a book, or saw a movie. But she did it herself, repeating me, me, me, all day long, like a goddam broken record. Like nobody else needed anything. Center of the universe, she was.

Eva smiles when she thinks about old Betty. She's a handful, Betty is, every nurse's nightmare patient. The kind who turns her TV on as soon as she's awake and leaves it at full volume until someone shuts it down around midnight. Goes without saying Betty keeps her finger on the buzzer, summoning help to fix her pillow or fill her water pitcher or pick her glasses up off the floor.

Not Eva—she never touches the patients' stuff, it's not her place.

The other day, a friend brought Betty some cranberry juice. Not one of those individual bottles, but a whole goddam half-gallon. Around ten o'clock that night, Betty got thirsty. She tried to pour some into her plastic cup. Spilled it, on her bed and all over the floor. Natch.

Eva had finished mopping the hall in her assigned section and was about to start on the operating rooms. They actually paged her, a cleaning woman, to come clean up the mess. Oh, not by name. She's no doctor. They just say 'maintenance' and the code, and if it's your floor you know to bring your bucket and cleaning cart and go.

Poor Betty sat in her bed, laughing and crying. Sometimes one, sometimes the other, or both at once; it was hard to tell. She sat there like a little kid, swinging her skinny legs over the side, big red splotches of juice staining the baby doll pajamas she had brought from home. Mascara streaked down her cheeks, mingling with traces of fuschia lipstick embedded into the wrinkles around her mouth.

The nurses wouldn't change her sheets until the floor had been cleaned.

The cleanup was a two-bucket job. The puddle started under the bed and spread all the way to the window. Eva didn't think those bottles held so much, and was surprised at how sticky the stuff was. *So much for no added sugar,* she thought.

"You want to send these home to wash?" Eva held up the sodden plush slippers, which had been ivory with white ribbon rosettes just a half hour ago.

"Nah. Toss 'em," Betty snorted, mid-laugh. "I got plenty more." She let out a wail, and fixed Eva with a doleful look. "I'm an oilman's widow. I got everything."

"That so," Eva mumbled. She thrust the mop all the way under the bed and swished it around.

"Yeah. He kicked off when I was forty. No kids. I couldn't have any, and he wouldn't adopt. I've been trying to spend the dough for the last thirty-eight years. It's not as easy as you might think."

Eva straightened, dipped the mop into her bucket and watched the reddish-gray stain swirl through the water. "So give it to charity," she said, her voice neutral. Who cared what rich people did with their money.

"Charity. You might as well flush it down the toilet, for all the good it does after they're done skimming off for this and that. I'd rather just give it to people, or spend it on shoes."

"You one of those big tippers, like Willie Nelson? I hear he leaves two, three times the bill sometimes."

"I can be, if they treat me right." Betty drew a finger across her throat. "Otherwise, nothing."

Eva wiped some juice splatters down from the bedside chair and wheeled her bucket to the utility closet for a refill. By one o'clock, she had finished with the spill and the operating rooms and took her lunch break, settled into one of the employee lounge's high-backed arm chairs.

What's it like to be Betty? she thought. She put her feet up on another chair, leaned her head back and closed her eyes. Was it better to be alone, doing whatever you wanted, no one to look after or answer to? She thought of her mother, who never blamed, never reminded her of even the gravest mistakes Eva had made, but looked at her with pity behind the sweetness in her eyes. And Mimi, who trusted no one, it was true, but you would think there'd be something, a little warmth, a daughter's occasional smile. Even if...

She sighed. If time healed, how long did it take? How goddam long?

At least Adam loved her. Adam loved everyone.

Eva was almost asleep when the page came again, cutting

through her drowsiness. She glanced at the wall clock: ten minutes left. *They can wait*, she decided. *For what they pay me, they can wait.*

In Betty's room, pandemonium ruled. The IV pole lay on the floor in a pool of clear liquid; the air smelled pungent, funky. Two nurses and an aide were trying to subdue the patient and restore order. Betty stood firmly planted at the bathroom's open door, feet wide apart like a ballerina in second position, the panties of her fresh baby dolls clinging wetly to her stick of a body.

"How long does a person have to yell before you lazy sluts get up off your big butts? Look, you made me piss myself! Don't touch me!" She shoved the aide hard enough to make the girl stumble and slip, falling with a hard *umph* on the floor.

Eva stood out in the hall. Nothing would get cleaned until all those people cleared out of the room. She watched the male nurse step behind Betty, grasp her by both arms and carry her into the bathroom.

"Let's get washed up," he said in his best nursey manner. "You'll feel a lot better."

"You!" Betty screeched. "I thought you were nicer than the others. I liked you! I was going to leave you money in my will. But don't hold your breath now, I've changed my mind."

"All right now," he murmured, and beckoned the aide to help with the washing.

When it was over, Betty in bed with a fresh IV and strict instructions to stay put, her hot pink nightie, ruffled at the neck and tied with a silver ribbon, glowing against sheets changed for the third time in twelve hours, Eva was finally able to clean the room.

She went through the mechanical motions she had performed who knew how many hundreds of times: sink, toilet, hand rail, shower, wall tiles. If she worked slowly, she could make the job last until her four o'clock break. She backed out of the bathroom, finishing the floor with rhythmic strokes of the mop, and was startled to find Betty watching her from the bed.

"What's your name?" Betty's voice was a hoarse whisper.

"Eva," she replied, and busied herself with the cart, making sure to leave no sponge, rubber glove, or cleaning product behind.

"Eva, do you smoke?"

"I quit a couple of years ago." *It got too expensive.*

"I'd give anything for a cigarette right now."

"I know how you feel." Eva pushed the cart out into the hall. "Believe me."

Betty cleared her throat. "Listen, Eva. Get me some smokes. I'll give you the money."

"What, now?"

"Not now. Tomorrow."

"I'm off tomorrow."

"Next day, then. Looks like I'll be here for a while, they're not done with me yet."

Eva was tempted to ask what was wrong with her, but didn't really want to know. "You can't smoke in the hospital," she said. "Even the staff has to go outside."

"Never mind that. I'll find a way. You just get them for me, okay? Menthol." Betty rummaged in her night table drawer, pulled out a beaded change purse. "Here, this should be enough." She handed Eva a ten, then added another twenty. "And that's for you. Take it, take it. I've got plenty more."

The bus going home was overheated, the air stale and metallic after the early morning freshness. Eva unbuttoned her coat, loosened her scarf. She studied the sky's cold dawning light, replayed the night's events. Why was life like that? Did anyone ever get all the pieces?

She thought of her gentle father, who had truly loved her. What if he had not been worn down by undeserved, unimaginable pain, what if he had not been taken from her when she was not quite sixteen? Her mother had been happy in her marriage. Why did it have to end so soon, leaving her alone with her memories because no one could ever replace her Leo? And Joe, would Joe still be Eva's husband if he had not had the optimism, the hope crushed out of him? Would money have made enough of a difference?

What's wrong with me? Joe, her mother, Mimi—why was it so hard to get along with people? And why was there never any money? *Will I ever finally catch a goddam break?*

So here was Betty. Betty has all the money, and what of it? When had she stopped living and become defined by her power to dispense or withhold funds according to a system of her own invention? The Cashier of Happiness, who has none herself.

What do I know about it? Eva caught herself up. Maybe it was a mistake to believe love was the answer. Maybe love was a human invention, an arbitrary measure used to separate the deserving from the insufficiently selfless. The sheep from the goats. Maybe love was an idea promoted by the greeting card industry, to great financial profit. You can fix anything with the right card, a new toy, a special dinner, a trip, a dozen long-stemmed roses.

"No, you can't." She pressed her cheek to the cool window. "Some things you can't fix."

Elsie's Hut is less crowded than she'd expected on a Saturday night. It's a bar crowd, dominated by a party of noisy young people seated behind several tables pushed together against the back wall. A few middle-aged couples, regulars, Eva guesses, who come to dance to the jukebox or occasional local band. Tonight, there's a piano player at the upright, an old man with gnarled yet supple fingers who sings show tunes and standards at half-voice, as if to himself, punctuating the vocals with bits of jazz improvisation.

Eva slips onto a bar stool between two couples: on one side, two men study the menu with serious attention; on her right, a graying man with a much younger woman. *There's always one of those*, she thinks with a smirk. She understands an older man's desire for young flesh, but what about the women? Wouldn't they rather play with someone their own age? *Whatever. Leaves us 'mature ladies' out in the cold, though.* How long since a man even looked at her? Years.

Elsie's at the end of the bar, chatting up the customers; her fresh-out-of-the-bottle russet curls catch the light, bobbing in time with her ready laughter. The barmaid at this end is young. She wears tight jeans and a black skinny-strap top; long silky hair swings around her bare shoulders. She walks past Eva several times, taking orders, bringing refills. She stops in front of the guys on Eva's left.

"Catfish is good tonight," she says, smiling. "And the chicken Florentine. Comes with spinach."

"I don't know. Maybe I'll have the lobster ravioli, and a salad," one of the men says to his companion. "You?"

The barmaid starts to reply, but catches a gesture from Elsie—a quick chin-thrust. She looks up at Eva. "Oh! I didn't see you there. What can I get you?"

"Yeah. I know," Eva says. *Nobody does, honey.* "A beer. And the menu, please."

Holy cow, she thinks. *When did Elsie get so trendy? Twenty bucks won't cover it, not if I want another beer.* She sighs. "A burger, then. Medium well." She had sworn off red meat years ago, but she's hungry and nothing else fits her budget.

"Fries?"

"Sure, what the hell."

The food comes on a square plate, trimmed with sprigs of watercress, a tomato slice on a lettuce leaf, a pickle. There's car racing on the TV with the sound turned off. May/December, on her right, seem engrossed in the action on the screen, she nestled into his shoulder, his beefy freckled hand resting on her thigh.

Eva eats, watches. The cars go round and round. The piano player strikes up a familiar tune, but she can't catch the words. She finishes everything, even the watercress.

"Another beer?"

Eva nods. She feels odd here, an alien dropped into a strange world. *Beats sitting home alone, Eva.* She takes it slow on the second beer. She can't afford another.

"You like car racing?" the man next to her says. The two guys are gone. She looks at him, startled, as if someone had pierced her invisible shield.

She turns back to the TV. "Not much. Nothing happens. They just chase each other around, like a video game."

Just then, one of the cars veers off to the side, flips over twice. The wheels spin in the air, the engine smokes. "There. Something happened," the man says.

She looks at him again, closer. He's sixtyish, with thinning blond hair combed back, a little long around the ears. Could use a shave. "You mocking me?" Eva's eyes wander to his slightly wrinkled plaid shirt, the cowboy hat slider of his bolo tie. She's not sure of his tone.

"No. Just that nothing stands still. Something's always happening."

They talk some more. He buys her another beer. "You live near here?" He lays cash on the bar.

I walk the bride and her mother to the door. "Thank you. Don't forget to send me a picture."

Hell, I would have kissed them on both cheeks and paid their cab fare. They seemed happy with the bottle of Prosecco from my special-customers' stock, the one I keep for wedding party orders. Wedding trade has been good; it's almost time to pick up another case. I should give them real champagne, Moet, I suppose, or at least Korbel, but I'm not that crazy.

"Well, that's a nice piece of change." Gunther picks up the check and waves it around like it's too hot to handle. "You sure it's good?"

"It's good."

"What did she buy? Hammered gold?"

"Silk charmeuse for ten floor-length gowns, topped with fingertip chiffon capes. Pillbox hat frames, covered to match. It didn't hurt when one of the thin girls dropped out and the one who replaced her was a size sixteen."

"And the bride?"

"Satin, of course, in that new ivory shade, the one with pearly pink undertones. Looks like the inside of an oyster shell. Hundred and fifty dollars a yard. Chantilly lace train and headpiece. And a whole lotta tulle."

Gunther whistles through his teeth. "I hope the groom knows what he's getting into."

"I hear he's a banker, and not so young. Money to burn." I straighten up the counter, re-shelve the tulle. "Look at this linen. Came in this morning. Perfect for summer trousers, don't you think?"

"You know me too well, Mimi." Gunther sighs. "Yes. Cocktails on Fire Island, paired with a Hawaiian shirt. Perfect is right."

It's almost closing time. I wait on a couple of teen girls buying ribbon to match their prom dresses, answer the phone. It's Granna.

"How are you feeling, Granna? That's good." She's been a little tired lately, doesn't like this humid spell of unseasonably hot weather. "I'm out for dinner. Will you and Adam be okay? Make some of your special pancakes, he likes that."

Gunther motions *go ahead* for the linen. I put Granna on speaker and measure out two yards, cut and fold.

"Pancakes, good idea. I think I have some strawberries, too." Granna's voice fills the shop. It sounds cheerful, but a bit more wavery than usual.

"Do you need anything?"

"No, dear. Well, I have enough milk for the pancakes, but I could use some for breakfast."

"I'll pick some up. See you later."

Gunther puts the linen roll back in its cubicle. I love the way he moves—no wasted energy, every motion clean and spare, like a dancer.

"We'd be so good together, you and me," I say. "Are you sure you don't like women?" I hadn't meant to say it, it just came out. We've known each other too long for doubt.

"You're not a woman. You're my friend."

"Well then, friend. Come to Paris with me later this summer, once the busy season ends. Strictly business." I put the check in the bank deposit bag.

He looks at me with that little half-smile.

"I'm serious. It's been six, seven years since my last trip. Time to see what's going on, taste the air, as they say. I'll even throw in Brussels, for lace."

"Make it Amsterdam, and I'm there. I'll pay the difference."

"We'll see." I ring up the linen. "That's forty, after your discount."

Gunther looks stricken. I'm not sure if it's mock-shock or the real thing. "Business is business," I say. "But dinner's on me. Sushi?"

EVA

There isn't much kissing. What there is tears through her like a brush fire igniting the shredded remains of her hesitation. Eva hadn't remembered how it feels to have a man's tongue in her mouth, didn't think it had ever been like this. Her body responds, shocked into raw desire.

"Where's the light?" he asks, one hand brushing the bedroom wall. He crosses the room, opens the window a few inches. Eva frowns, but doesn't protest.

"No light. Please." She knows what she looks like—thick in the middle, her breasts too soft, her legs a road map of red and blue veins. "No light." She throws back the blankets, wishes for a moment she had changed the sheets.

It's all businesslike; they both know the score. He buries his hands in her hair and pulls, hard, yanking her head back and making her eyes sting with tears. Does she like it so rough? She doesn't know, because of the thing in her that comes up to meet him, open, hungry. It's been so long. She's like wine past its prime left undisturbed too long in the bottle. His deliberate movements stir up the murky sediment with a turbulence that makes her head spin. She strains against him, against his unyielding chest and thighs. His callous fingers play her until she no longer knows the word for what she's feeling. Elation? And also an ache that pulls at her guts, just this side of pain. Is there a difference?

He rolls off onto his back. "You okay?" he says to the ceiling.

Eva grunts. *Yeah*, she wants to say. *Okay like I just stuck my finger in an electric socket. That kind of okay*. It's overwhelming and at the same time, not quite enough. She can't talk about it.

She pulls up the sheet and turns her head to the window, where the light from the streetlamp inserts its beam between the panes of her flowered curtains. *I hate those curtains*, she thinks. She fights the urge to jump up, naked, strip them off their rods and trample them under her bare feet, but she lacks the energy.

They lie, shoulders touching without intimacy, not speaking. He reaches for his shirt, takes out a pack of cigarettes, lights up.

Eva finds her voice. "This is a non-smoking house."

"You can put up with it for five minutes," he answers, his voice cool but not unfriendly. "I won't be staying."

No, you won't, she thinks, with neither animosity nor sadness. *Why would you?*

She watches him tip a long ash into the cupped palm of his hand, studies his profile—the sharp nose, small ear, thin lips. He could be a rodeo performer or one of those guys who builds bridges, walking the girders with intrepid assurance hundreds of feet in the air. "What do you do?" She suddenly needs to know.

"Me? I drive an escort car, for wide loads. Been all over the country."

"Hm." She pictures him steering the advance compact car, warning flags flapping, a piece of house or boat or concrete highway divider lumbering behind, indifferent to the aggravation of dozens of motorists piled up in its wake. Do trucks still use CB channels to talk to each other? Anyway, he'd be in for the long haul, tuned in to country music or talk radio or maybe—why not? NPR. She knows for sure he won't ask about her. She won't have to say, "I mop hospital floors at night."

He gets up, carries the glowing stub of his cigarette into the bathroom. Eva hears water running, then the unmistakable sound of a man pissing in the toilet. She pictures him standing, feet apart, watching the stream raise a froth of yellow bubbles that float and burst against the sides of the bowl. It's strangely comforting to hear the ordinary sounds of a man in her apartment, her bathroom. *You've gone over the edge, Eva*, she tells herself. *Get a grip.*

She must have dozed. The next thing she knows, his hand is on her hip, his erection prodding her side. She turns to him, expecting a kiss, a caress. None comes. She feels his grip on her shoulder, a quick hard embrace, her breasts crushed against his chest. Then he is shifting her over, her face in the pillow. Pinned under his legs, his hands holding her wrists, she tries to say, "No. Not like this," but he is stronger, and he isn't asking.

When he falls asleep, Eva gets up. She squints at the bathroom mirror, sees the coarse, disheveled steel-gray hair, the dark skin pouched under tired eyes, the neck hung with loose wrinkles. Her body throbs, her heartbeat is wild, erratic; she opens her mouth and inhales deeply, feels her ribs expand until it almost hurts. *It's only hormones*, she knows. *Calm down.* She cleans herself up, washes her face, rakes wet fingers through her hair. "Who would have thought," she says to her reflection. "The last time in your life you get laid, you'd get fucked in the ass."

Really, Mom, she can just hear Mimi say. *Do you have to be so crude?* But there's no other way she can say it, without getting all clinical about it. He'd pleased himself while she lay there, face down, unable to look at him or respond. *What would you call it? Anal intercourse? Please.* As if she could ever say any of this to anyone, especially to Mimi. As if his being a stranger weren't enough.

What had she wanted, really? If things haven't turned out the way she expected, that was nothing new. Things happened to her, one after the last, marking her time into the shapeless semblance of a life. She's disoriented, sore, but that will pass, the whole incident becoming yet another thing to put away into that place where the unspeakable is kept. It isn't even the pain, the sharp flame that still smolders somewhere deep inside, that she regrets. What is it, exactly, she has just lost? Her dignity? No. Strangely, laughably, it is her innocence.

Back in bed, she lets waves of exhaustion numb her mind. He shudders, turns on his side, away from her. He's a quiet sleeper, his breathing broken now and then by a sigh, soft as a child's. This is the part she's missed in all her years alone: the animal warmth of a man's body, the tacit affirmation of her place in this moment of shared space. Even with the total absence of tenderness. *Take it for what it is*. She pulls up the covers and sleeps.

Not for long. She is aware, through waves of increasing wakefulness, of his stirring. He coughs a long, loud, hacking cough and sits up. Eva forces her eyes open. 3:25. The sky between the curtains, though still dark, is no longer impenetrable; it has that early morning quality, a kind of lifting or lightening, as though something is ending while the next thing has not yet begun.

"I'm going," he says, his head half-turned in her direction.

"Want coffee?" she asks his back.

"Yeah. OK."

She fills his mug, then watches him pour half down the drain, add milk up to the rim and stir in a spoonful of sugar. "Light and not too sweet, that's me," he says, with the closest thing she has yet seen to a smile. *You said it*, she thinks. She looks at him, aging, balding, not bad-looking. Ordinary. Alien. Unknowable.

Then she is talking, unwinding words that have spooled in her mind for who knows how long, words she had intended to keep to herself forever. "I didn't mean to hit her. Not hard, anyway. Not more than once. She stood there, right next to the potty, her panties already soaked. Pink ones, with little bunnies on them. When she heard me come in, she looked me straight in the eye and pooped into the panties on the floor. I'm not a monster, I know it happens. It was the eyes—nothing in them, no surprise, no guilt, no fear, nothing. Just ice.

"Sure, I'd hit her before. She was a stubborn child, already thinking she could have things her way, and her not yet two. I'd smacked her butt when she needed it. That's what I meant to do, smack her butt to teach her a lesson.

"I couldn't stop. I guess it was her defiance; she absolutely refused to be good, made my life hell every day. As if it wasn't already, after Joe walked out and left me with nothing but debts and emptiness. My hand came down, again, again. She tried to run, got tangled in the panties around her ankles, fell down, howled. God forgive me, but there was a sick satisfaction in hearing that screaming, as if I'd finally got through to her, as if for once I was in charge. Me. 'Mommy,' she blubbered. 'Mommy.' I didn't care. The rage kept pumping through me, moving my arm up and down. I didn't care where my hand landed. I couldn't stop."

He lights a cigarette, sits with his mug in both hands.

"My mother lived on the same floor, next door. She came in, picked her up, took her away. We didn't speak to each other for almost a year, my mother and I. I couldn't look at her. I turned my back if we met on the stairs. If she said anything, I ignored her. I was ashamed.

"Small as she was, my daughter never called me Mommy again. She became guarded, independent, cool. She showed me every day how little she needed from me.

"Finally, my mother said she would kill herself, go drown in the river, if I didn't start talking to her. I knew she was serious. She does what she says. So we talk, but everybody hates me. And I deserve it."

He takes a long drag, gets up and douses the butt in the sink. "Look," he says. "You gotta sort that shit out. You know about reincarnation? Well, I don't know what you believe, but if there's another life for you, it ain't gonna be any better than this one. We don't get but a couple of chances to set it right."

She looks at him. There's a hint of softness around his mouth, a glimmer of—something—in his eyes. She knows there won't be time to find out what it is.

When he's gone, Eva remembers what he said, in the bar, a thousand years ago. *Nothing stands still, something's always happening.* "Fucking philosopher," she says, stripping the sheets off the bed. "Know-nothing Zen master. Set it right, my ass." In the dawn light, she scans her room with revulsion. These objects—the dresser, mirror, lamp, her uniform on the ironing board—he might have looked at them, they might have absorbed the fleeting attention of his indifferent gaze. They are complicit, contaminated, mute witnesses that turn her foolish lack of judgment into humiliation.

And the curtains! The curtains most of all, rippling with every frigid breath of the winter air. *But you liked it, Eva*, they seem to murmur, hanging there all innocent in their flowered vanity. *Admit it. You liked it.*

She bunches the smug cloth in both hands and yanks. The rod clatters to the floor, brackets and nails and even a piece of loose plaster. She slams the window shut. Crossing the room, she exposes the other window somewhat less fiercely. "This, I can do," she says. "Now." She kicks the whole mess into the kitchen and stuffs it into a garbage bag.

She calls in sick that day; Betty will have to wait for her smokes. *You can't always get what you want,* Eva hums. *Or, be careful what you wish for. Or some such bullshit.* She wraps herself in the quilt from Adam's cot, curls up on the couch and sleeps until hunger wakes her well past dinnertime.

"What's wrong with your bed, Grandma Eva? There's no sheets on it. And your curtains are missing."

Mommy went to the movies with Gunther and some other people, and Granna has a cold, so I'm sleeping over, because Grandma Eva has the night off from her job. Grandma Eva doesn't say anything for a while. She's busy knitting something long and brown. I think maybe she didn't hear me, so I try to ask again. Her bedroom looks so strange, I really want to know.

"What's —"

Grandma Eva sighs. "I have to turn the mattress. You can help me, later." She knits some more.

"Oh," I say. "OK." I open my crayon box to find the right color for the dog in my coloring book. Not black. I hate black. I could use a rusty color, but I lost that one. Maybe it could be a storybook dog, red or blue or green. That might be fun. Then I find the brown one. "Look, Grandma Eva, it's the same as your —" I hold the crayon next to her work. "What are you making?"

She pulls it away from me. I wasn't going to color it! Then she looks at me and her eyes get kinda crinkly, but she's not smiling. "It's a blanket, for my bed." She shows me a basket with some finished pieces. It looks like a big bowl of chocolate pudding, only it's feels like a sweater.

"Are you making new curtains, too? What's for dinner?"

"Fish sticks. Carrots." She knits. "Potatoes."

I color the dog. It has long ears and a big fluffy tail. It's called a Lab-ra-dor. I can't read the other word, but Grandma Eva looks grumpy so I don't ask her. I go to look out the window. It's snowing. Everything is already white, the cars and everything. There's even a little hat of snow on top of the streetlight, across the street. I want to go outside, but Grandma Eva is cooking, so I don't say anything, I just set the table. That's my job.

Dinner is pretty good. I even get to have some ketchup with my fish sticks. Grandma Eva only takes a little, because it's not healthy. Me, I like ketchup. The carrots are plain. When Granna makes them, they taste like dessert. Maybe one day Granna can tell Grandma Eva how to do that. I don't say anything, she might get mad. I just dip them in my ketchup.

What I don't like is the green stuff she puts on top of the potatoes. I try to push it off with my fork, but she catches me.

"When will you learn to like parsley? It's good for you."

I make my sad face.

"OK, Adam, just this once," she says. She moves my potatoes to her plate and gives me some plain ones, with butter. Wow, that never happened before. I always have to eat everything, at Grandma Eva's.

When we finish cleaning up—my other job is to dry the silverware and put it in the drawer, in the right places—I put on my pajamas and we watch a video. It's about a dolphin named Flipper and the two boys who are friends with him. It's pretty cool. I was getting kinda tired of watching *Charlotte's Web* all the time.

Then Mommy calls. I hear Grandma Eva say, "Yes, it's really coming down. I'm sure school will be closed. Yes. All right. We'll be there by noon." She hands me the phone. "It's your mother," she says, and goes into the bathroom. I know that, I'm not a baby!

I tell Mommy about the video, and the snow. Then I whisper, "Grandma Eva put pars on the potatoes, but I didn't have to eat it." I talk really fast because I hear the bathroom door opening.

"What? I can't hear you," Mommy says.

"Never mind. We have to go turn the mattress now," I say,

louder. I'm not sure what it means, but it sounds important. "Bye."

Turning the mattress is hard. We have to pull the head end toward the feet, so it's like upside down. Then we have to turn it *over*. Grandma Eva does that part herself, it's too heavy for me. I'm just a little kid.

"Will you put sheets on it now?"

"No," she says. "It needs to air out some more. I'll sleep on the couch."

I don't understand. It looks like a regular mattress, why does it need air? The couch is hard and lumpy, that's why she got me a cot to sleep on when I'm here. There must be a grownup reason.

In the morning, I'm all excited to go outside, but we have to eat our oatmeal first. I stand by the door, all ready to go, while Grandma Eva looks for her gloves. She puts on her boots—black ones, with some fur coming out of their tops—and wraps a scarf around her neck. She puts another scarf on her head and ties the ends under her chin. I'm glad my coat has a hood.

The snow is great. It's the fluffy kind, that squeaks under your shoes and shines like magic dust. Grandma Eva has her shopping bag, so I know she needs to go to the store. She walks on the sidewalk, on the shoveled part. She takes little steps and keeps telling me to be careful.

I'm a snow hare. I turn my head one way, then the other, using my long pretend ears to listen for danger. Dogs? Foxes? Arctic wolves? At least I know the grizzly bears are sleeping. But there could be hunters. I stay in the deep snow, at the edge of the sidewalk. In my mind, I make my feet big and flat. Thump. Hop. Thump. Sliiide. The snow's up to my knees, though, and it's really hard to keep hopping. So then I'm a polar bear. I take big steps, one foot at a time, and think about catching a nice fat seal for lunch.

At the store Grandma Eva buys some milk, shredded wheat (yuchh), and bananas, and some meat with yellow SALE stickers on it and a cabbage. I'm glad I'm not staying for dinner. Cabbage is my worst food.

We stop at the thrift store on the way home. It smells funny in there, like old shoes, and most of the toys are broken. Grandma Eva finds a big old sheet with blue and white stripes. She makes me hold one end while she opens it up. It has a rip on one corner, and a couple of little spots. "I can work around that," she says.

We fold it back up. "Is it for your bed?"

"No. I'll use it to make curtains."

Grandma Eva buys me a box of animal cards. It's a matching game. I'm too old for that, but the pictures are cool, even if one rhinoceros is missing. I put the game in my coat pocket, so I'll have something to do while Mommy's working. We take everything else home, then go the other way to Mommy's store. I hope she bought pizza for lunch.

Now I'm only a boy, walking in the snowy city. Grandma Eva holds my hand.

ANNA

So Mimi's off to Paris. Good. She's always working, putting all her energy into that shop, staying late to meet customers who just can't seem to make it during the day. The only place she ever goes is New York City, for the annual fabric show, and to visit showrooms and shop in the garment district. I know for sure she hasn't had a vacation since before Adam was born.

It's a hard life, running a business, raising a child. We help, Eva and I, but she carries the burden, the worry. Adam's a sweet boy, but no child ever grew up without sickness or some kind of trouble. Take my Eva, for instance. I swear she was born unhappy and determined to stay that way. Who knows why? Her life is full of longing for things she'll never do, and regret for the ones she's done.

Well, that's another matter. No point dwelling on it.

Adam's starting to ask questions. "Granna, how far away is my daddy? Will he come back soon?"

I tell him to wait a bit, and then we go make pudding, or read *Wind in the Willows* or something else with animals in it. It's possible he has a *Papa*, not a Daddy. Mimi came back from her last trip six years ago, full of ideas. That's when she opened the shop. But she won't say, and I'm only guessing.

She's excited about going—I know that much.

The other day, we were having coffee in that nice little Greek place around the corner from her apartment. Adam was at a birthday party, a Sunday matinee. Greek coffee is black and strong and sweet, just the way I like it. I don't care what Eva says about caffeine and whatnot. I take my heart pills, so leave me alone.

Mimi was drinking iced tea with mint. "Gunther has a great

eye," she said. "He can spot a trend about to hit before anyone I know, better than any stylist or designer. Why he's snapping pictures for a living is beyond me. He'd make a killing in the rag trade."

"Who knows why people do things?" I said. "I'm glad you're not going alone."

"Yeah. And he's fun, too. Curious about everything. Talks to strangers. Gunther can make a party happen any night of the week" She rattled the ice in her glass, got up to go. "Gotta go get the boy. Thanks for letting me use your suitcase, Granna. I'll pick it up in the morning."

I almost got to Paris once. Leo was always talking about it, always meant to go to practice his French. I'd known him since sixth grade; we met in—you guessed it— French class. I watched his infatuation grow through the years. He loved everything: the food, the movies, poetry, art, theater, wine. He read everything, from Dumas to deBeauvoir, and especially Montaigne, whose essays he practically memorized. He probably drove the guys at work crazy with his favorite quote, *Que sais je?* What do I know. Or this one - How many several ways hath death to surprise us?

He even liked that hokey French accordion music.

It was endearing, really, except for the times I felt like screaming if he recited any more Voltaire, or hummed another note from *Carmen*. He knew I liked to read murder mysteries, though, especially those set in Paris. So I guess I fanned the flames, so to speak; I was complicit, even if I didn't share Leo's obsession.

What is it about beautiful, romantic Paris that inspires so much crime writing? The French are full of contradictions. Cool passions. Catholic guilt and the art of the love affair. Joan of Arc and *Can-Can*.

"Just think," he said to me once, years ago, during one of those daydreamy moments he was prone to. "We could be in a bistro, enjoying a glass of Beaujolais with our *soufflé aux champignons*, listening to Edith Piaf. And there, at a corner table, we'd see Brigitte Bardot dining alone, reading Lamartine. We'd recognize her in spite of the scarf and sunglasses, but like everyone else, leave her alone. Until Charles Boyer came and sat down with her. Then the girls would come. You know how they follow him around."

"Really?" I laughed. "Too bad he's dead, and she's never been shy of publicity. And you can't read anything in a bistro while wearing sunglasses. Besides, aren't Lamartine's verses too old-fashioned for such a glamorous movie star?"

"Brigitte is a country girl at heart," Leo nodded, his expression grave, wise, and smitten all at once.

"So when are we going?"

"Soon. Let Eva finish high school and find a job. Then we'll go." He turned the page in his *Paris-Match*, then put the magazine down on the table. "I'll be retired in ten years or so, collecting my Roto-Rooter pension."

I knew that. I also knew that our chances of getting to Europe, let alone seeing Brigitte Bardot, in a bistro or anywhere else, were pretty slim.

He would never see that pension, never celebrate Eva's graduation. He'd never witness his daughter skip from one dead-end job to another, always last hired/first fired, while lurching from one hopeless boyfriend to the next.

It would have broken his heart.

Or he might have talked her into taking a class, picking up a trade. She might have listened to him. She might have learned more compassion. My words had no effect on her, not then, not now. Except maybe the once.

Instead, forty years of smoking those stinking unfiltered Gauloises finally did their worst to Leo's body, God damn it. *Vive la France.*

This is the way I'll always remember Leo: he's lying on the couch, propped up with cushions. His sharp knees stick up under the crocheted blanket like *papier-mâché* Alps in a diorama. I'm sitting on that chair with the awful orange upholstery, right next to him, holding the atlas on my lap.

"Why stop with Paris?" he says, tracing his finger along the map of western Europe. "Or even France? What about Belgium, Switzerland, Monaco? Luxembourg."

"Luxembourg? Do they speak French there?"

"We could look it up. I'm pretty sure they do." He closes his eyes. His breathing slows down; I see his shoulders sag. I start to close the book.

"Don't go," he says. "I'm just thinking. After Europe, we could go to Africa. What do they call the Congo now? Zaire. Or is it the Democratic Republic of Congo? Yes, I think so. And there's Senegal, Mali, Benin, Ivory Coast. Haiti, Polynesia..." He drifts off.

I watch him relax. The yellow skin of his stubbled cheeks sinks against the bones of his face. The hollows under his eyes look bruised in the dim lamp light. The post-chemo tufts on his scalp tremble with each breath.

He never did snore, my Leo.

Croissants are a divine invention. I can't eat one without hearing Granna say, "Your grandfather believed the secret ingredient was arrogance." Maybe he was right. There's something about the balance—butter to pastry, air to essence—that smugly implies, don't even try to do this at home.

Gramps would only buy the ones from the French bakery, La Vie Parisienne, two towns away but worth the trip. Even Granna said so.

I wish I had known him. He sounds like a real character, a philosopher in work clothes. Olive drab twill, maybe, with his name stitched over the shirt pocket. I wonder if he was content, cleaning out drains while thinking about, I don't know, Molière or something. Maybe we don't need to satisfy every desire. Maybe a little yearning is a good thing.

Besides, he had Granna, and she's as cool as they come.

She doesn't talk about it, but it must have been hard looking after him, putting on a cheerful face, watching him die.

Gunther and I did talk about it, somewhere over the Atlantic, the night clouds like shifting gray cushions under our wings. Another one of his friends had wasted away, the chemical cocktail nearly as brutal on his body as the disease.

"I don't know if I could do it," I said. The wine in my glass was tepid, too sweet. I was in no hurry to finish it.

"You'd be surprised what you can do," he answered. "For someone you love."

I tried to imagine what that would be like. Oh, I could visit, sure, and read aloud, or give them music to listen to and good things to eat. It's the other part, the bathing and turning, the diaper changing, the withering and helplessness I don't think I could stand.

I'll never tell Gunther what happened that one time he asked me to sit with his lover for an hour while he did errands and picked up Chinese for dinner. Larry, the one with all the funny stories. Everything went great, me feeling appreciated, useful and good.

I read to him from *Alice in Wonderland*, his choice. When we got to his favorite part: 'Never imagine yourself to be otherwise than what it might appear to others that you were or might have been was not otherwise than what you had been would have appeared to them to be otherwise,' he chuckled and asked me to read it again.

Then he said he had to pee. Okay, I said. You have to help me, he said. Help you get up? No, he said. Hold me. My hands shake, he said. It took a long time, the hot piss dribbling into the bottle while he lay with his eyes closed, as if guiding his dwindling energy to this vital task. His shrunken, spongy dick was cool and dry in my hand. I'm sorry, he said.

It was too much. I was angry. With Gunther, for not having warned me; with Larry, for allowing the fucking scourge to ravage his body; with modern medicine for not being willing to fix it, now. With myself for feeling inadequate and ashamed.

"I guess I've never loved anyone enough," I said. I held up the diminutive airline snack packet. "Want these? I'm allergic."

He tore open the little bag, scattered peanuts all over his tray and picked them off one by one. "You love your family. Your mother, your grandmother. Adam."

"Adam's a child. Of course I could care for him. And Granna's strong enough to look after herself. Mom, though, let's just say it's complicated. I'm not sure which one of us is deficient when it comes to love."

But back to croissants. I almost laughed out loud the first time I saw four *gendarmes* at the take-out counter of the corner café pick up their morning usual. They didn't even have to say anything. Four *cafés au lait*, four croissants, money on the counter. *Merci bien.* If I were a writer, I'd store that scene away for sheer delight, find a use for it somewhere.

"So where to today?" Gunther cuts his croissant in half, lengthwise. He smears strawberry jam on one side, Nutella on the other, takes alternate bites. It's a two-handed job, his head moving to nibble first one, then the other. Right, left, right, left.

Not me. I like to deconstruct my pastry, unwind the layers to expose the flaky crenelations, still warm from the oven. Seductive and vulnerable, both. "I thought I'd cruise the wedding shops, for starters, see what they're showing. Wanna come?"

"Maybe for a bit. Wedding shops are so dull—all those greedy-eyed salespeople preying on nervous brides and their happy mothers. Or happy brides and their nervous mothers. It's all the same. I'd rather stroll the Champs-Élysées, see what the fashionable people are up to." He watches me drizzle honey onto a strip of pastry. "I wonder what our breakfast habits say about us."

"Huh." I polish off the croissant and lick the honey off my fingers. "I like to get to the bottom of things, and you want it all, I guess. Anyway, it's July. The fashionable people are in Tuscany or the Riviera. All you'll see is tourists."

Gunther finishes his coffee, sets his cup down precisely in the middle of his saucer. He leans in and winks at me. "Tourists can be fun too, Mimi. But it's still early. The interesting people tend to linger over breakfast while they consider their day. I'll give you two hours."

Adam

I'm such a lucky kid. Mommy and I always have fun together. I miss her right now, while I'm thinking about her. She said, "I'll be back soon, Cowboy." She calls me that sometimes. Soon can be a long time, when grownups say it. So I get sad, too.

Before she went away we went shopping. She bought some things for her trip, and I got new shirts and shorts and sneakers. We had hot dogs for lunch. "Don't tell Grandma Eva," Mommy winked at me, "or we'll both be in trouble." Then we walked around with our ice cream cones and looked in all the store windows. It was okay, but a little bit boring, until we got to the pet store.

They had kittens in the window. There was this box with round holes in it, and the kittens would go inside and pop their heads out of the holes. It was funny. Then they jumped around and rolled on the floor. I wanted to do that, too, but the sidewalk was dirty. Besides I'm almost six.

One kitten, the one with the black ear, got tired of playing and went to sleep. Just like that. Bam. "I like that one," I said. "Can we take it home? I'll call him Pirate. Please?"

"Sweetie, you know we can't." Mom always calls me Sweetie when she's serious. "Grandma Eva doesn't like cats, and Granna, well, it just might be too much for her."

"When you come back. Can we get him then?"

"We'll see," she said.

"Yeah." I took a big bite of my cone, the cookie part, and my ice cream fell out, splat, on the ground.

Mommy threw her own cone in the garbage. "Let's go to the bookstore."

That was fine. We got a story book called *Abel's Island*, about a mouse, and one called *Animals of Australia*, with lots of pictures. Plus, some new coloring books—dinosaurs and jungle animals— and a box of crayons.

"Did you know that in France the word crayon means pencil? They say it like this: kre-yon. *Crayon*."

"*Crayon*," I repeated.

"When I come back, I'll bring you some nice colored pencils, the kind French children use. Okay?"

"Yes Ma'am!"

"And do you know what French children call their mommies? They say, *Maman*, or *Mama*, sometimes. You can call me that, if you want. Just don't call me Mama Mimi."

I giggled all the way home.

Anyway, here's why I'm so lucky. Granna got me a hamster! She said another boy in her building had a whole family of them, and there were too many babies.

I love my hamster. He has light brown fur, kind of like peanut butter color, a white tummy, big black eyes, a pink nose, round mousy ears and funny little feet. And whiskers. I wanted to call him Henry, because, well just because. Granna said, "What if it's a girl? We don't know for sure. You could give it a fun name, like Fluffy or Skippy."

"I have to think about it," I said. I didn't want to call it Fluffy or Skippy, but I don't like to hurt Granna's feelings. Then I got an idea. "Lucky. I'll call it Lucky."

We went to Target on the bus to get Lucky a real hamster house, with hamster toys and wood shavings, a water bottle and special food. He doesn't have to live in a shoe box anymore. It's dark in there, and Granna said he could bite a hole in it with his sharp little teeth and run away, or he could die from having nothing to do. Now he's happy.

I sleep at Granna's while Mommy's gone. We share her big bed. Lucky likes to play all night, spinning in his wheel and running around, making tunnels in the wood shavings (Granna calls them *bedding*) and crunching his special cereal. We don't mind. Granna says she doesn't like to sleep a lot, anyway.

In the morning she takes me to day camp. Grandma Eva picks me up at lunchtime. We have soup or chicken nuggets with vegetables, or something else healthy. And grapes or an apple. Apples are all right, but I really like candy, too—jelly beans or green M&Ms. And chips.

Grandma Eva lets me watch a movie while she takes a nap, and then she brings me back to Granna's and gets ready to work at the hospital. She works all night, while other people are sleeping. I wonder what that's like. Maybe Lucky would understand.

Lucky and I play together every day. He sits in my hand and lets me pet him. Then he runs up my arm and across my shoulders. He has tiny claws that prickle my skin, but it doesn't hurt. I still think he's a boy, like me, even if his name isn't Henry.

The other day, after dinner, Granna was reading *Abel's Island* to me. Abel is a mouse who has to live by himself on an island after a big storm. I really like that story, the way Abel has adventures and learns to take care of himself, and gets out of trouble by being smart and brave. Granna explains some of the hard words, like *maelstrom* and *marooned*. I like that, too.

We were sitting on the sofa, like we always do. Then the door opened and Grandma Eva came in. "Eva," Granna said. "What's wrong? You look pale."

Grandma Eva sat down in the big soft chair and put her bag on the floor. I could see the top of her paper lunch bag sticking out. Under that I know she carries a black sweater, and under that, at the bottom, her blue coin purse and a comb and some tissues. She eats the same sandwich every day, rye bread with turkey and lettuce, no mayo. And a pickle. She likes pickles. She calls it her night lunch, which sounds kinda weird, but I guess she's used to it.

"I don't feel so good," she said. "The bus hadn't come yet, and I had to sit down."

"What's wrong?" Granna said again. "Adam, get your grandma some water."

I went in the kitchen and filled up a big glass and brought it to her without spilling any. Lucky sat on my shoulder the whole time. Grandma Eva took the glass. Her hand was shaking a little, so she spilled some water on her working dress. It's called a *uniform*.

"Oh," she said. "Damn." Her face was white and sweaty. She drank some water, then put her head back against the chair and closed her eyes. "I think I ate some bad fish. My stomach feels queasy, and my back aches like a son of a bitch."

I don't know what *queasy* means, but it sounds bad.

"Eva, why did you come up all those stairs? You could have called me." Granna was frowning. "Maybe you should go home. Lie down."

"I don't know, I can't think straight. I'll just sit here a minute. I can catch the next bus." She looked at me and her lips made a straight line. "Why isn't he in bed? It's after eight."

"It's summer, Eva. Relax," Granna said. "We were reading a story."

I held up *Abel's Island*. "See, Grandma Eva, it's about a mouse, and he gets *marooned* on this island all by himself, and I have a hamster, see? His name —"

Grandma Eva made a funny noise, like she was trying to say

74

aaah and ugh at the same time. "Don't you bring that ratty thing near me. Just finish your story and go to bed."

Granna started reading again, the part where Abel starts feeling lonely and wants to go home. I started to feel sad for him, but then Lucky climbed up my arm inside my pajama sleeve, came out behind my ear and jumped on top of my head. He was combing my hair with his paws. It really tickled.

Granna stopped reading. "I'm sorry," I said. I thought she was mad at me for not paying attention. "Lucky —"

But she wasn't listening. She dropped the book on the floor and stared at Grandma Eva.

Grandma Eva looked terrible. Her face was gray like the baby koala in my new animal book. She was shaking. She dropped the water glass and wrapped her arms tight around her chest. She tried to get up, but fell on her knees and then down on the rug. Thud.

Granna got down on the floor too. She put her mouth on Grandma Eva's face, like they were kissing, then pushed with her hands at my grandma's chest. She looked up at me with big scared eyes.

Lucky got scared, too. He ran away and hid behind the sofa cushion.

"Adam," Granna said. "Call 911. You know how."

And I did.

EVA

She doesn't feel sick, exactly, just so, so tired. There is no pain, not like the bolt that had seemed to split her back in two, leaving her helpless, gasping. When her knees hit the floor, the shock wave had traveled up her legs, into her arms, her neck, her jaw. She will always remember the terror.

Then the hospital. Someone has taken charge of her body, decided what will drip into her vein, how fast, how long. Her body is wired to send blips and squiggles telling somebody somewhere she is still alive. Air tubes up her nose help her breathe. As if she, Eva, is missing, and only this damaged vessel, which needs to be repaired, remains.

No, not missing. People come by, talk to her about annoying things in false voices. How do you feel you're looking better look you have company. She feels reduced to a poor sum of her parts, each one examined for needed adjustments and treated according to its basic function. *And isn't that a good thing*, she thinks, when thinking becomes possible, *that there are people who know how it's all supposed to work. Hallelujah.*

Once awareness returns, she can't stand being in the hospital. She hates the fussy vigilance, the endless checking of vital signs, as if she were a school science project to be monitored and reported on. There is the interminable boredom. Television helps pass the time, but sometimes watching the clouds drift past her window provides more distraction. Sleep is numbing but not restorative; she wakes feeling restless, day and night, as if she needs to be somewhere else, doing something important.

The cleaning women are the worst part. How can these lazy sluts live with themselves, knowing they left dirty streaks and dusty corners in every room? She can imagine the bathroom, is glad she can't see the smudges on the faucet.

Life has not given her too many lucky breaks, but she has always done her best. Hasn't she? In every job, she was the best: the most careful envelope stuffer, the most thorough night-shift grocery shelf stocker, the most accurate inventory taker, the most efficient gas station convenience store clerk. The best floor mopper. She is not a perfectionist, no. She only knows she has to try harder, giving no one the right to criticize her for lack of effort or write her up for poor performance. She needed those goddam stupid jobs, knew only too well how many other people stood ready to scramble for them if she stumbled, failed. When, invariably, each job ended or businesses moved, went bankrupt, automated, that was not her fault.

She had been a good mother, too, damn it. Except for that one time, that crazy thing that came from, well, who knows where crazy things come from. Some raging monster raises its head out of your special personal hell and takes over, and then you do something you regret for the rest of your life.

But she had always provided for her family of two. They always had a place to live, the nicest clothes she could afford, enough food. Every year, she went to school to meet Mimi's teachers, to hear all those things she already knew about her willful child. There were toys, too, and books and whatnot, though her mother had helped with that a lot, taking Mimi to shows and museums. And why not? That's what grandmothers do.

Is that so? She can hear the Bullshit Monitor echo somewhere in the depths of her mind. *Like you do for Adam?* "Shut up," she mumbles. Adam is in no way deprived, and Mimi has her own ideas, doesn't need Eva's bolstering to make a good life for him. He is happy, doesn't demand or expect more from his grandmother than she is able to give. She's nobody's fairy godmother.

So what the hell is Mimi's problem now? She has an education, smarts, a firm sense of direction. Like the father she never got to know, she's struck out on her own. But she's not poor dumb Joe, she made it work; she's giving her life the shape she wants from it. She and Adam seem so happy together, so complete. Eva hadn't imagined raising a child alone could be so uncomplicated. Whatever the story is with the boy's father, it's clear Mimi doesn't need him around. So what is it? Does Mimi even know why she continues to begrudge her mother any shred of affection? How much can she possibly remember?

You've got to sort that shit out, the guy said, before he put his coffee mug down and walked out the door. No kidding, Einstein. As if Eva doesn't know where the thorn lies, the splinter buried under years of silence. As if she can't see how bright and funny Mimi is with Adam, how caring with Anna, her grandmother. Only when it comes to her mother, Mimi is a blank, all feeling concealed behind her impenetrable shield.

The guy. He never told her his name; she never asked. He wasn't so bad, though. She'd liked the hard, lean look of him, the straight back, smooth shoulders. He must have shaved before going out to the bar, but by early morning there was enough beard to raise a light rash on Eva's neck. That was all right, she kind of liked it.

She liked, too, the way he hadn't run right off, stayed a while, slept. The sex was a little nuts —fast and rough. Even that was all right, finally, though she couldn't say she liked it much. It's just what happened, that's all. It had been so long, years. She no longer knows her body that way; maybe that's the way it is when you get older. Things get dull in the middle, sharp around the edges.

In the predawn light, he listened while she talked. Well that was decent, wasn't it? Who knew why she started talking; maybe because he knew her in a way no one else ever had. Or because he didn't know her at all. Not even her name.

She only knows that some dam had broken, some kind of barrier had been removed, and words came flooding out. She hated his calm superiority, his cool moral sureness. Her fury had been a way to hide how much her heart hurt to tell it; she knows that now, had probably known it then, too. But stripping the room had been grand. No need to analyze that, it was the most alive she'd been in ages. "At least you got new curtains out of it, Eva," she smirks into the room.

The cleaning woman glances at her but says nothing, continues to wipe down the windowsill. Be sure you get the underside, too, Eva wants to say, then thinks, *Fuck it*. It's her head on the platter if she does it wrong, not mine. She lets her eyelids close.

Yeah, telling it, to anyone, brought a kind of relief. But it was like sealing her confession in an empty bottle and tossing it into the waves—it's out there somewhere, but so what? What good is it if none of the people it affected knows anything about it? There's something more she has to do.

She drifts off, carried by the drone of constant buzzing in her head. Then it is night. Outside, no moon, no stars that she can see in her square of sky. In the dim hall, the faint squeak of rubber-soled shoes advance, pass her doorway, retreat. Someone laughs. Somewhere nearby a hoarse, pitiful voice calls out "Nurse. Nurse!"

All at once Eva's mind clears, wiped clean of confusion. "Where was I?" she says. She struggles to catch the thread of her last thought. Something, something. Oh yeah, something she has to do, about Mimi.

It would be like starting a knitting project without instructions. She has the yarn, the needles, some vague idea how the finished piece will look. Without a pattern, though, she's not at all sure how to get started, how many times she might have to rip the stitches out and begin again. How long it will take. Whether, once it is done, it will fit.

But if she does nothing, it will just fester where it is, a tangled, shapeless mess under a pile of accumulated stuff that presses it, flecked with lint and dust and too much regret to ever be of any use, into the bottom of the basket.

"I can't fix it all myself," Eva says.

A nurse comes in with medication, chirps something inanely cheerful. Eva swallows obediently and lets herself sink once again into deadening sleep.

When she wakes, Anna is there, slumped in the chair by the window.

"Ma," Eva says. "How long you been here?"

Anna stands up. "A few minutes." She smiles "I brought you a magazine. *People*. There's not much to choose from in that gift shop."

"I know. Kittens and bears. Still, better *People* than *Car and Driver*. Thanks." She gestures toward the window. "What's it like out?"

"Not too bad, after yesterday's shower. It'll be hot later, though." She rummages in her handbag. "I thought we'd trim your nails. It looks like the nurses' aides don't get around to it."

Eva reaches for the clippers. "Let me." She tries to position the cutting edge against her thumbnail, but even resting her hands on the rim the bed tray is not enough to still their trembling. She lets the clippers clatter onto the tray. "Damn it," she says without anger. "Guess you'd better."

"Okay." Then, "Done. Here, use some of this while I do your toenails." Anna squeezes a smear of lotion from the hospital-issue bottle into Eva's palm.

It is odd to have someone, anyone, touch her feet. Anna spreads a hand towel on the sheet; her touch is deft but gentle, her hands cool and dry on Eva's blanket-warmed skin. Minutes later, Anna gatheres up the towel, shakes the clippings into the wastebasket. She wraps her hands around Eva's right foot; her fingers press into the calloused pads, working the hardened sole.

"Do you remember what you said to me once, when you were little? No, of course not, how silly of me. You couldn't have been more than three." She spreads some lotion on her hands, picks up Eva's other foot. "You said, Mommies wipe you and cut your nails. That's what Mommies do."

Eva's head sinks into the pillow. Eyes closed, she lets herself go with the rhythmic pulse of her mother's massaging hands. How can a person be overwhelmed yet utterly serene at the same time? The thought flashes through her mind, followed by blissful emptiness. There is only this sensation, this act of kindness which is, she realizes, the single most intensely intimate experience of her life.

"No shit," Eva mutters. "I said that?"

I don't believe in reliving the past. It's not my style.

We don't meet again in the same café. That only happens in romantic novels. I do go back to La Bonne Chance, sure, why not? There, and a dozen other spots I remember from my last trip, seven years ago.

No, I see him purely by accident, outside a movie theater, in the center of a group of people blocking the sidewalk. He's the one talking, his round face aglow, one hand in midair, making his point. The others—two, three men and a couple of women—seem content to serve as audience.

I don't need to hear what he's saying. I am sure his views are punctuated with Do you see? It's obvious. *N'est-ce pas?*

Talking with him had been like that. If you had an opinion, his mission was to bring you around to his way of thinking. The Stones were a good band, sure, but the Beatles changed music history. Basquiat may be full of fire and rage, but he's undisciplined; Warhol's flat, cool canvases are the true expression of modern times. How can you not agree?

I didn't, hadn't always agreed, but I hadn't argued, either. I was only a few years out of school then. What did I know? My trip, a gift from Granna for my twenty-fifth birthday, had been a stream of revelation, like a mind-bending baptism into an old new world. Or a new old world, I don't know which. He had been only one piece of it. An important piece, yes. But not as important as he probably thought.

I guess I hesitate just long enough for him to glance my way. "Mimi!" he calls out. "Mimi, is that you?"

He crosses the street. We stand a moment, appraising each other. He looks much the same, only his hair is cut shorter, styled by a fashionable barber's hand. The baby fat I remember from our last meeting has solidified into a permanent pleasing plumpness.

I wonder how I look to him, whether he notices the faint lines etched around my eyes and mouth. "Hello, Étienne," I say, as if seeing him here like this is part of my itinerary, the most natural thing in the world.

"Are you here long? Have you had dinner? I know a nice new place just out of town, three stars." He is all energy, his eyes bright and piercing as ever. "Wait, let me say goodbye to my friends."

"No, no," I say. "Can't we join your friends? I've been here three weeks and hardly talk to anyone, except for business."

"*Mais non*, they are too dull. Wait here." He runs across, comes back, and steers me toward the car.

The car. I don't know how I could have walked past this unique machine without recognizing it. A seagreen Citroën convertible, roof down, immaculate inside and out. The special-order walnut console, equipped with enough clocks and gauges to please an aviator, gleams in the gathering dusk.

Am I ready for this, for riding once again wherever he wants to take me? The cap, the driving gloves, the self-satisfied profile?

"I saw a *brasserie* that looked inviting," I say. "Can't we go there? It's only a few streets away." There it is, the pleading note in my voice I'd been determined to avoid. Maybe he didn't hear it.

"A *brasserie*? Really?" His hand, on the flank of the car, wipes at dust only he can see. "Well, if that's what you want..." Then his face lights up like Adam's with a new picture book. "You know, I just replaced the engine. After looking many months, my mechanic found one in excellent condition. So my car is *comme nouveau*.

How do you say it? Like new." He reaches for the door handle.

It's all too familiar. He is bending my will, knocking the sense out of my head. Again. I feel the air thin out, as if only *his* breathing matters.

I have neither the mood nor the budget for three-star dining, with its four-course ritual, its wait staff's barely masked condescension steeped in faux-servility. But I have eaten every meal alone since Gunther left for Amsterdam. And I am, strangely enough, glad to see Étienne. What I need is some backbone.

"Yes," I say. "The *brasserie*. It's what I want. It's a fine night, though. Let's walk."

The *brasserie* is exactly what I expected—comfortable atmosphere, reasonable prices, unpretentious house wine, good simple food. If Étienne doesn't like it, tough.

"Are you still editing?" I break the crust off my bread and dip it into my soup, ignoring the scowl clouding his face. *I'll just be myself, okay?*

"Yes. But no more freelance. I work for a publishing house now." His expression brightens by degrees. It happens to all of us, doesn't it, when we talk about ourselves. "Often I can work at home, in my studio."

"Poetry?"

"Ah. Poetry. No. I have learned I am no poet." He spreads mushroom paté on his bread and takes a small bite, reminding me that we are, after all, in Paris, not in an American roadside diner. "I edit art books for children. Also sometimes biographies of famous people in history—you know, Louis Pasteur, Alexander the Great, Madame Curie."

"You like it?"

"It suits me, and pays enough." He refilled our glasses. "And you? You are in *couture*? Fashion? Was that not your interest?"

"Not exactly." The restaurant is warm. I undrape the scarf I finally learned to wear the way French women do. "I met some manufacturers when I was here, got to know something about fabric. When Adam started kindergarten, I opened a small shop." *Damn.* I hadn't meant to mention Adam. It just slips out.

"Adam? Your son? You are married, then." He glances at my hands, at the elaborate dragon ring on my right index finger, the skull-and-crossbones on my left pinkie.

"No."

"Divorced?"

"Single."

"Ah."

We eat. Perfect veal medallions, roasted potatoes, crisp baby *haricots verts*—to call them green beans sounds almost insulting. I polish off everything on my plate, finish the bread and salad, too. Étienne leaves a few bites of rice pilaf and fish, motions the waiter to take it away. I had forgotten that habit, how much it annoyed me. He is a child of privilege; my mother tolerated no waste. I hadn't needed, then, to be reminded of the class gulf between us.

Now I don't care.

"How long will you stay? Have you seen much of Paris?"

"You know I'm no tourist. I only go to museums to study the clothes in the paintings." I laugh. "I'm visiting bridal shops this trip."

"Bridal shops? *Vraiement*? You plan to be married?"

"Never. I go to see what brides and their mothers will be wearing the next year or two, so I can be ready." I stir my coffee. "And I walk a lot, look at the people."

He insists on paying, then suggests we go to his place for a cognac. Guest in my country, old times, blah, blah. As if I don't know how it goes, how European men think buying a woman dinner gives them unassailable bedding rights. *Sometimes dinner is just a meal, between friends*, I want to say. Are we friends? Had we ever been?

I beg off, invent an early appointment, try to look truly sorry. I don't want to see those rooms again, the red leather sofa, Persian rug, deceptively humble metal bed with its big square pillows and cashmere blankets. No. Even if all those things are gone. Maybe especially if they are gone.

That night I lie on the bed in my little attic room, the cheapest single the hostel has to offer. The window cut between slanted eaves offers a view of some of Paris' celebrated rooftops, the tiles gray under half a moon, the chimneys stalwart, tall and dark. Pigeons settle in the crevices and perch in rows along the crests.

My mind is blank. Maybe I doze a little—it's hard to tell, things seem so unreal. To be in this place, where even the shabby spaces have a bit of chic, even the ordinary has some magic about it. *Cut it out*, I tell myself. *You're falling for the hype.* I stare at the ceiling, see, in the dark lit by the distant glow of a streetlamp below, patches of peeling paint. The leaky faucet at the tiny sink in the corner drips; the window is spotted with the previous day's rain.

Étienne. My hand on his back, my fingers finding the mole, there, nestled in the hollow next to his spine, my eyes open to the ferocious gentleness in his face. The kiss. Oh, the kiss, the first one. You can make love with the same person dozens, hundreds of times, but you're only seduced once. And it's delicious.

"Stop it, Mimi," I say. "Don't forget the other part." No meaningful conversation, by summer's end; the passion mechanical, the wonder gone.

I get up, stand at the window. In the next house, one floor

down, a hand appears at the open window, empties the contents of a yellow teapot into a window box of geraniums. The flowers look shadowy, like in an old black and white movie; the leaves catch a silvery glint of reflected moonlight. A lamp goes on in the next room. Someone's torso in red-striped pajamas walks through, the head obscured by the angle of my line of vision. A woman's voice floats up. "*Ah, oui. Merci.*" Then dark.

Étienne and I meet one more time, at an art store he has recommended. I buy a box of colored pencils for Adam, a journal with the Luxembourg Gardens in spring bloom for Granna. Nothing for Mom, not in an art store. I'll look for a nice collapsible umbrella, maybe, or something else practical, at one of the street bazaars. I bought chocolate, at the confectioner, but can't remember what kind she likes.

"This is for your son," Étienne says when we part. "A book about animals in art. For Adam."

As if I don't know who my son is, have forgotten his name. "Thank you," I say. "He loves animals."

We look at one another. No handshake, no farewell kiss.

Adam

It's me who tells Mommy about Grandma Eva.

Granna and me are coming back upstairs after taking out the garbage. We always take the garbage out together. Granna says I'm not old enough to do it by myself, because the garbage cans are in the basement and I'm not allowed to go there without her. I know where they are, and where the light switch is, and everything, but grownups always have a reason why kids can't do things. I wonder if there's a rat down there, like the one in *Charlotte's Web*. I'm not sure if that would be cool or scary.

I don't really do anything, except maybe turn on the light and open the stinky garbage can, but Granna says she likes my company. "Hold your nose!" I say, like always. Phew.

So anyway, we're coming up the stairs and we hear the phone ringing. Granna says, "Go answer it, Adam. It's probably your mother." It is.

"Hi, Mommy," I say. "When are you coming home?" I always say that, and she always says, "Soon."

"You didn't call yesterday."

"I fell asleep," she says. "Then it was too late. I'm sorry, Cowboy. Hey, where do you think pigeons sleep, here in *Pahree*?"

"I don't know. Where? But guess what? Grandma Eva fell on the floor and had to go to the hospital. She had a heart tack. That's what the ambulance man said, I think." Granna is still in the hall, but the door is open, so I yell, "What's a heart tack, Granna? I forgot."

She comes in all huffy like the big bad wolf and closes the door. She takes the phone from me and says, "Pajamas. Now." She gives me that look people get when they want to talk about something you're not supposed to hear.

I leave the bedroom door open a little bit. Granna says, "Yes, Mimi. That's right. She's in the hospital." She listens, then says, "Stable, they said, but weak. You should come back. I'll tell you more when you get here. These calls are expensive for you."

She sits down. "She wants to come home, says she can't stand the sloppy way they clean the room. She wants to get out of bed and show them how it's done." She listens again while Mommy talks.

"Yes, I know. Pride in your work is good, no matter what the task. But it upsets her. She'll be calmer here."

Then Granna looks at the bedroom door. Maybe she can see me standing there, inside. Maybe not. I didn't turn the light on, but it's not real dark outside yet. She turns her back to me and says, "It'll be hard for me, with the boy. Come."

And then she hangs up. Click. I never get to find out where pigeons sleep, in Paris.

Eva

She feels like that blonde in the movie, the blonde with the red-painted lips, who screams and squirms in King Kong's hairy paw, terrified by his bottomless lustful eyes. The movie is black-and-white, but she knows the lips are red just the same. They have to be, on a floozy like that. *Fool*, she thinks, *you think it'd be better if he let you go, dropped you from the top of the Empire State building? Leaving your lovesick beau to gather your bloody broken carcass into his grieving arms.*

But it's a movie. Once you create a beast, you can make anything happen. And people watch it with shivery delight, before returning to the ordinary horrors of their own lives, where monsters tend to be bureaucratic clerks drunk with the power to dispense food stamps.

These thoughts come to her later, in the ambulance, with the plastic mask from the oxygen tank covering her nose and mouth. *Ask not for whom the siren wails*, comes to her stupidly. *It wails for thee.* It would have hurt too much to laugh.

Before that, there were only the huge leathery fingers squeezing her rib cage. Her lungs burned for air; the breath caught in her throat like a swelled cork in a bottle, unmoving. She remembers lying on the floor, the ceiling of her mother's living room as far away as the sky. The room was dim—was it evening? The twin lamps threw large yellow suns that shimmered around the edges before fading into the gloom of unlit corners.

There was Adam, his smooth little-boy face floating above her; his expression showed fear mingled with fascination. His lips moved, but she heard nothing, the words an echo coming to her minutes later: "Grandma Eva, Grandma Eva."

Another voice, "Get me a blanket, Adam."

"This one, Granna?"

Her mother's face replaced his. Eva could see the wrinkled cheeks, the sagging pleats under her chin, the worry in her eyes. Why was it so cold? She felt cloth pressed to her forehead, her mother's hand warm against her skin. Then nothing, until the fog lifted a little, confident hands taking her, tucked and strapped like an Indian baby—what was that called? It was, for some reason, very important to remember. *Chinook? No, starts with a p...papillon, parapet, pontoon? Think, Eva, think.* They bumped and rocked her down the stairs and outside, where a cool misty rain, persistent and gentle, bathed her face. "Papoose," her mouth formed the word that nobody heard.

She wakes to daylight, the sun striping a pale-green wall through partly lowered blinds. Anna sits in an armchair near the window, an opened notebook on her lap, her head back, eyes closed. *Damn, she's old,* Eva thinks. *When did that happen?* She studies her mother's face as if looking at a stranger, notes the creased skin, the deep purple pouches under her eyes. The slack jaw, a thread of drool forming at the corner of her open mouth. *Pale as a sheet.*

Eva feels her heart stir. The crushing pain is gone, replaced with a gnawing ache that seems to outline all her joints and muscles, as if she's been beaten with a stick and left, bruised, to die. "Cut the drama," she says. Twin tubes inserted in her nostrils pump air to her lungs with each breath, the apparatus gurgles like a fish tank she once had, long, long ago. She focuses on the IV, the substance entering her vein one hypnotic drip at a time. Four-...five...six....Behind her head, she hears the bleep of machinery. A heart monitor? Most likely. The beats subsided a little, the bleeps came in a more measured rhythm. Seven…eight….She doesn't fight the blackness that passes for sleep, sinks into the abyss.

She comes out of it to see Anna standing by the window.

"Where's Adam?"

Anna jumps. "Oh. You're awake. He's charming the volunteers down at the visitors' desk. How do you feel?"

Eva dismisses the question with an anemic wave. "Hare-brained do-gooders with time on their hands, those volunteers. Bring him up."

"How —"

"Leave the pass here, and all your stuff. Get him and come back up, like you know where you're going. Use the stairs instead of the elevator if you're nervous."

"But Security…"

"Security's a joke. It's a community hospital, not a prison, Mom. You watch too many movies." Her voice fades to a whisper, as if she were allowed only so many words at one time and her nickel has run out.

He comes in all scrubbed and scared-looking, and again she feels her heart stir. *This is all I've got. These two people. And Mimi. Well, yes, Mimi.*

Adam holds back, then seems to make up his mind. He steps forward and stands next to the bed. "Hi, Grandma Eva. Are you okay? What's that box with the lights and squiggly lines? It looks kind of like a robot."

"Hush," Anna says. "The box shows the nurses how your grandma's heart is beating. No more questions now."

"Oh. We made clay animals at day camp. Look, I did a walrus." He holds out a brown lump on the palm of his hand. "I used a little stick to make the skin wrinkly and splooshed the tail flat with my fingers. But I couldn't make horns or whiskers, and one of the flippers fell off."

"Nice," Eva nods.

Anna slips an arm behind Eva's shoulders to turn the pillow. Eva sinks back into its coolness, dizzy with exhaustion. "Let's go, Adam," Anna says. "Grandma Eva needs a nap."

"Okay. You can have my walrus like a present, Grandma Eva. Even if it's not your birthday." He sets the figure on her nightstand. "You can look at it when you wake up."

They are mopping the floor. Eva knows the sounds. Dip, squeeze, swish. Move the bucket. Dip, squeeze, swish. Each pass is accompanied by ragged, asthmatic breathing. Who is it? Eva runs through all the cleaning women she knows—the moppers—and comes up blank. She opens her eyes just as the woman straightens with a grunt and stands motionless at the foot of the bed, one hand pressed into the small of her back.

She is young, fresh-faced, Spanish-looking. *Latina*, Eva corrects herself. *We're supposed to say...ahh, fuck it*. What's the difference? Nobody mops floors and cleans toilets if she can do something else. Poor is poor.

This girl is clearly new, the way she grips the mop, underhand, like a tennis racquet in a match Eva watched on TV once. And she moves way too much, leaning into her strokes, tossing the mop head around so vigorously she leaves a pattern of dirty droplets on the baseboards. A do-over, for sure, if she gets caught by a supervisor.

"What's your name?" Eva strains, but can't read the tag without her glasses.

"Mona."

"Look, Mona. Do it like this," she motions her closer. "Damn."

She winces at the pain shooting through her arm. She tries to wrap her hands around the mop handle, but loses her grip. "Like this, see?" she pantomimes instead, waving her right arm in a wide arc, fingers curled down over a phantom handle. "And slow down. When's your shift end? Eight?"

Mona stares. She looks baffled and a little suspicious.

Christ, she's fresh off the boat, or the bus, or wherever the hell America's workforce comes from these days. "When do you go home?"

"Oh. Nine o'clock. PM." She speaks carefully, as if anxious to get it right. They both glance at the clock. Two-thirty.

Eva lies back. "Give me some water. There, on the tray. Thanks." Her head feels full of rocks; behind her, the monitor bleeps rapidly a few times. "Do a good job, but slow down, or you'll be dead by dinnertime."

"Okay," Mona says. She nods, smiles a little, and moves on to the bathroom. Eva turns on the TV, find a documentary and lets the narrator's drone lull her heartbeat back to normal.

When Anna comes, an hour later, Eva asks her to crank the bed up some. "Get me out of here, Mom. Take me home."

"Has something happened? I don't think you're strong enough yet." Anna sets her bag on the floor and sinks into the armchair. "Oof. It's hot and humid out, hard to breathe. You're better off in here."

"I don't mean right now. But soon. Real soon. Like tomorrow. Where's Adam?"

"At story hour at the library. My neighbor took him." She fans herself with the visitors' pass. "So what happened? Between Medicaid and Disability, you're fully covered. What's the hurry?"

"They don't clean right. No, really, don't look at me like that. See the corner, there." She tries to sit up, points at the floor near the window. "That girl missed it completely. If I did sloppy work like that..." All the goodwill she'd felt toward Mona evaporates in the heat of her desire to leave. As if, once home, everything will be like before. A week to recuperate, then back to work, and watching Adam, helping Mimi with the shop. She just has to get out of this place, where sick people linger, growing weaker by the hour. Or go crazy, like poor old Betty, shouting abuse at the staff before disappearing into some limbo where nobody cares if you live or die.

"Calm down. Here, sip some water. Now relax. They take care of you, don't they? Feed you and bathe you and bring your medicine? Change your sheets? Let someone else worry about the floor."

Eva lies back, turns her head toward the privacy curtain the last nurse had left partly drawn along one side of the bed. She stares at the design—schools of little multicolored fishes float randomly on a pale background. Blue blue pink pink pink yellow yellow black black. Then again, blue blue pink pink pink yellow yellow black black. Again and again, with tiny white bubbles rising from their mouths toward the unseen surface. Maybe her mother is right. Why worry about the floor? It isn't her problem. And who will do all those things for her, the feeding and washing and sheet-changing? *Well*, she thinks. *Isn't that what mothers do?*

She raises her eyes to meet Anna's. "Please. I want to go home. I want your soup, your cooking."

Anna puts the water cup down and folds her hands over her stomach. "You'd have to stay with me, at least for a while. I need to get ready. And I still have Adam. Mimi's due back Tuesday. I'll ask the doctor, but you have to be patient."

"All right," Eva saiys, her voice a hoarse croak that seems to scrape against her throat. "All right."

A nurse comes in, pulling a cart loaded with equipment. "The doctor wants another EKG," she says brightly. "Won't hurt a bit." She pulls the curtain all the way around the bed. The nurse works briskly, swabbing cold gel on Eva's skin, attaching electrodes to her body, turning dials. "I feel like goddam Frankenstein," Eva mutters. "And just as ugly."

She closes her eyes. Shapes of little fishes swim under her eyelids. Blue blue pink pink pink yellow yellow black black.

MIMI

*GUNTHER—GOING HOME MOM SICK MEET ME AT
ORLY GATE 23 9AM SUNDAY IF COMING—MIMI*

He almost misses the flight, of course. I'm relieved to see him bobbing through the crowd with less than five minutes to spare, a head taller than almost everyone else, his hair cut in a sleek new continental style.

"You could have changed your ticket, left from Amsterdam, you know."

"Honey, I'm so broke, I barely had enough for a mineral water on the train. I wasn't about to risk losing my seat home."

"Have a good time?" I ask. He just smiles.

"I love this part," Gunther says. He jams his bulging duffel into the overhead compartment and sits down in the aisle seat.

"Which part is that? The waiting, the scuffling, the last-minute negotiations with unruly children?"

"The sorting out. You have a crowd of people, each with his own reason to be here, her urgent desire to be somewhere else. And then it gets sorted out, matched up. Everyone in place, ready to go. It's so civilized."

"Glad you think so," I reply. "I think more about the ones left out, who come too late, or can't afford to come at all. The ones with fears and anguish, the lonely ones."

"Oh, stop. You're depressing me. Why the mood? Is is your mom?"

"No. Though it must be serious if Granna said to come." I settle in, look out the window at the circling utility vehicles, watch an orderly row of suitcases creep up a conveyor belt into the belly of a plane. "Just bummed."

Gunther says nothing for a while. I suck the dregs out of my coffee container, mashing its edge in with my teeth. He seems to be trying to decide if it's his business to ask; then curiosity wins out. "What happened, Mimi?"

"Nothing much," I stall. But who could I tell if not Gunther? "I ran into somebody I knew."

"Somebody...what? Stupid, rude, fresh? Must be pretty bad to frazzle your nerves so much."

"Somebody I met on my last trip. We were—"

"I get it. An old crush. You never know how that will go. So?"

I slip my shoes off and rest my feet on top of them. "Crush. I never thought of it that way, but I suppose that's what he was." I press down on the coffee container, flatten it with my hand. "You know, seeing it that way actually helps. Makes it feel more insignificant."

"So..." Gunther leans forward, turns his head to look me in the face.

"Oh, Gunther. I was so naive, on my own for the first time, far from home. I tried to act tough, but I was all emotional jelly underneath, ready for the first seducer. Étienne turned up right on cue."

He winks. "Tell me about him. We have a few hours. You know I need to know."

"That's just it. There was nothing exceptional; he didn't stand out from the Parisian crowd. He just happened to be the one who noticed me."

"There must have been something unusual. There always is, once you get past the small talk and the first date."

I smile at the tone of his voice, the suave expertise of a man seasoned in the art of the casual encounter. I have to give him something. "Well, let's see. There was the car. A sporty little number that didn't go anywhere without its daily bath. And, um, he didn't wear underwear."

"Ohhh. . . . Say no more." His hands rise in the air. "I know the type."

"Don't tell me," I laugh. "I don't think I want to know." Though, of course, I should have known. I should have recognized the narcissism, the inward focus that leaves no room for genuine feeling toward anyone else. It's not as if there's none of that *me first* imperative in my own makeup.

"So what went wrong?"

"I wish I knew. He was charming and sweet and French. It was lovely, at first. Kind of innocent and urbane at the same time. I thought, well, this is nice. I wasn't schooled in love affairs, didn't know anyone who had moved on to the next phase, whatever that may be. Not anyone I could talk to."

"Were you in love?"

I have to think a moment. "No. I believed I was, at the time. I said the words. But no." I hand the flight attendant my mangled cup, accept a small apple in return. The apple fits perfectly in the palm of my hand; I hold it absently, feeling its cool skin warm up to the touch of my curved fingers. "What did I know? Even those of us who claim to be independent turn out to have very ordinary expectations. You meet someone and then *this* happens, and then *that*, and *that*, and so on. You're just like everybody else. And it seemed okay."

"Honey, I know what you mean. But the fun part is in the surprises, isn't it? Even if the surprises break your heart."

I glance at him. Sometimes Gunther just makes no sense at all. "Maybe for you. For me, there was no fun, and the only surprise was how quickly things changed. The sex became routine, and the only thing he could talk about was his beloved old *tante* in Monaco—her herb garden, her fish pond, her watercolors, her recipe for onion soup."

"Classic." Gunther seems delighted. "For a narcissist, there's always someone else in the picture, not just you. Someone who appreciates them more than you ever can. Were you jealous?"

"I was bewildered. How could I deal with this third person, this old woman I'd never met who was always in the room with us, or just outside. As if she was sitting in her favorite chair or in the back seat of the car and, I don't know…knitting." This sounds so absurd. I make a pathetic noise, something that starts like a laugh and ends with a snort, a hiccup.

Gunther leans back in his seat. Maybe I've unleashed too much melodrama, even for him. Maybe he's sorry he asked.

"I'm sorry…" I start to say.

"But he loved you, if only for a little while," he interrupts.

That's an easy one. "He loved his car, Gunther. His little green convertible."

"And the Monaco auntie?"

"I'm not sure. He told me he hadn't visited her in years. I think she sent him money, some kind of allowance or something. Maybe the memory of divine onion soup is better than a bowl steaming in front of you."

We stop talking. Gunther checks out the movie options, picks out a comedy. I close my eyes, think wearily about Mom and Granna and the drama waiting for me at home, my fingers still wrapped around the apple. My mind conjures Adam's baby-smooth face, his pointy chin and spiked hair, his grave, insatiable wondering about the world. Damn, I miss him; I only now realize how much.

After a while, Gunther chuckles and turns off the screen. "So Mimi," he says. "How did it end, with Étienne?"

"We had a date. He didn't show. I went home."

"Just like that?"

"Just like that. When I'm done, I'm done. I move on. When I saw him last week, I learned his aunt had died, he'd left for Monaco in the middle of the night. But really, what's another hour if she's already dead? He could have come, right then, in the middle of the night, or called. He could have treated me as if I mattered."

"You didn't stay in touch." It's not a question.

"What for?" *Maybe this was one of those surprises that breaks your heart*, I think. But that's going too far; I know my vanity had been engaged far more than my heart. "I was mad as hell. At him, but really with myself, for not recognizing a commonplace dalliance when I stumbled into it. My mistake, believing the smooth words sprang from anything like true feeling. I couldn't see us becoming transatlantic penpals." I snap my tray into place, recline my seat back a notch. "What for?"

Gunther picks a stray hair off his shirt sleeve. He flicks a crumb off his knee and folds his hands in his lap. "Is Étienne Adam's father?"

I open his hand and place the apple in it. "This is the worst part of the trip," I say, my head turned to the window. "There's nothing to see but clouds."

ANNA

"Are you sure you're able to do this? Your daughter—" the social worker glances at the file on her desk, " —Eva will need constant care." She looks at me over her glasses as if evaluating my stamina.

I sit up straighter. "How long? The constant care, I mean."

"It's hard to say. The doctors say her condition is stable, but her body's had a major shock and she's still very weak. She'll need help with bathing, dressing, personal hygiene, special diet. Really, a few more days here would be better."

"She wants to go home. I'm sure you know that keeping her here against her will can make her sicker. I can manage."

I want to ask her what she knows about constant care, how many sponge baths, adult diapers, salves, massages, medications have been part of her life. Does she know the trick of hiding extra butter, olive oil, sour cream in every bowl of soup or oatmeal, so the few spoonfuls that get eaten carry maximum calories? How many nights has she spent on the couch next to a rented hospital bed, listening for breath, afraid to close her eyes, until sleep finally wins out and she wakes to nothing but the ebb of tires on wet pavement through the open window, as if mocking the dead silence in the room. How many people she loved have left her without saying goodbye? *You never know*, I remind myself. *Suffering is not always written on the face.* "I can manage," I repeat.

The social worker leans forward, hands folded on top of the file. "Medicaid will pay for thirty days recovery in a nursing facility."

"Out of the question."

"All right then." She opens a drawer and extracts several sheets of paper. "Eva also qualifies for a home health aide, someone to come in and give you a hand." She slides a form across the desk. "And this is a requisition for equipment—oxygen tank, commode, wheelchair—already approved by her doctor. And a visiting nurse twice a week for the first month. Just sign here."

She is beginning to get on my nerves. I have things to do. I sign.

Mimi's flight is delayed by bad weather. That leaves Adam and me to do everything. You wouldn't think there was so much to it, bringing a sick person into your home. Just change the sheets and make sure you have plenty of chicken broth and camomile tea. It's not that simple.

We make many trips, Adam and I, between Eva's first-floor rental and my third-floor condo. We still live in the same building, though it's been many years since we'd been neighbors on the second floor. Now she occupies the only unit deemed not worth converting when the building went condo. Tucked into an odd-shaped corner at the end of the hallway, under the stairs, its bathroom is not much bigger than a utility closet, which I suspect it had been at one time. But the place is cheap. I expect she has grown used to the overhead stair traffic, has learned to ignore the tired footfalls or cascading hurry of people with places to go, while she sits in that chair with the worn gray upholstery, watching television.

I'll never know how she got so much stuff into those three dismal rooms. An alcove near the door serves as both coat and broom closet, her winter boots next to the mop and pail. The furniture, well, "vintage" would be the kindest way to describe it. In the bedroom, which at least is big enough to turn around in, her clothes hang on a metal rack in the corner; Adam's cot leans against the wall, its legs folded out of the way. By the bed, a stack of old magazines, health and, strangely enough, travel— discards from the hospital waiting rooms. The dresser is a paint-it-yourself project, now dingy beige, with at least two other colors showing at the chipped corners.

We take three nightgowns and all her underwear, plus a bathrobe and a sweater, pile them in her laundry basket along with some sheets, pillowcases, a blanket and some towels. Adam races upstairs, one pillow under each arm. I follow at my own speed with the basket.

There isn't much in her refrigerator: some yogurt, a stick of margarine, a few slices of whole wheat bread, a cucumber and a couple of soft tomatoes. Adam cradles the food bag, his face framed by two houseplants sticking out the top. "Not so fast, now, Superman," I say. "or we'll end up with a bag full of mush." His ready smile melts my heart.

I take his folded cot into the hall, turn off the lights, lock the door. Trudging up the stairs, I have to stop two or three times to catch my breath, wondering once again why the committee decided against installing an elevator. Finally, I just sit down on the second floor landing and wait for my eager helper. "Take one end," I instruct, but he grabs onto its edge with both hands.

"I can do it, Granna." He pulls and slides the cot all the way to my open door, me a step or two behind to catch it if he lets go. "See?" His grin is broad and self-satisfied.

We take a break for ice cream, with strawberries and chocolate chips. "What about Lucky?" Adam asks, licking the back of his spoon.

"Hamsters don't eat ice cream," I answer. "But he might like a strawberry."

Adam laughs. How I envy children their laughter, the way they fill a room with merriment, honest and unrestrained. I know that the same intensity is true of all their emotions: sadness, anger, or blackest despair. That doesn't stop me from wishing I still knew how to laugh from the gut, how to clear the accumulated debris of everyday living from my mind, conscious of nothing but the clarity of joy.

"I mean," he says, still giggling, "do you think Grandma Eva wants to keep Lucky in her room? She doesn't really like him."

"He makes too much noise, especially at night. Grandma Eva needs to sleep, so she can get better. Let's put Lucky here, in the kitchen, until your mommy comes. Then you can take him home with you."

"Okay!" Adam jumps up, comes back with the hamster cage. He takes Lucky out, holds him in one hand and strokes him with a gentle finger. The little beast looks up at him. I don't know that you can read expressions on a hamster's face, but I believe something passed between them, something perhaps as simple as love.

Adam puts Lucky down on the table, in front of a strawberry the size of a walnut. We watch the hamster sniff the fruit, whiskers twitching, then anchor it with his front paws and sample a leaf. Soon enough his face is buried in the aromatic flesh, devouring the treat in quick, small bites with enthusiastic grunts and whistles. "He'll be licking strawberry juice off his fur for the rest of the day," I predict. I get up to answer the doorbell. "Put him away, now. You can leave the cage here, on the counter."

I ask the delivery man to place the oxygen tanks at the foot of the bed, like two four-foot sentinels ready to dispense their life-giving commodity on demand. The commode goes in the corner, behind its own privacy screen. "What's that?" Adam lifts the seat cover, peers inside.

"A commode. Like a potty for grownups." For once, he has no

answer, his eyes wide, mouth open, taking it all in. The wheelchair is the folding kind; that fits in the closet. I don't think we'll be using it right away.

"Will you sleep here with Grandma Eva, like you do when I stay over?" His arms are full of clothes I am moving to empty a drawer for her. "Is the cot for me?"

"The bed's for your grandma. I'll sleep on the couch and you get the cot, in the living room. She'll be here tomorrow, so let's finish putting these things away and order something for dinner. Chicken or pizza?"

"Chicken," he says, to my surprise. "With mashed potatoes and gravy. No peas!"

"All right. I'll call, and you clean up the hamster poop on the kitchen table."

"I already did," he says.

Mimi

How odd it is to have run into Étienne. And how, at the same time, fitting and necessary. Everything is clear now, the parts that were a mistake, and the parts that weren't.

Close that door. See what's going on at home.

It didn't sound good, if only because Granna had said so little. She can handle anything, I know, so it's hard to tell when things may be too much for her. As for Mom, well, she's a bit of a whiner.

Gunther calls a friend to pick us up at the airport, who takes his time showing up, but at least we don't have to empty our pockets to get home.

I put my bags down and call Granna.

"Oh, Mimi," she says. "You're back." She sounds small, far away.

"How's Mom?"

"Sleeping. She's sleeping. Adam, too."

"And you? How are you?"

"Oh, fine. Fine. Did you just get in? What time is it? Why don't you get some rest and come in the morning."

It's just past nine—too late for dinner, even if I had wanted any. There's sandpaper behind my eyes, my sinuses are full of wet cotton. I start to unpack. A shower, and bed, and I'd be good as new, ready for whatever is waiting for me over there. Something keeps nagging at me, though. Conscience, maybe. *What?* I want to say. *What?*

But I know well enough. I stayed away too long, took my time coming back. Maybe I shouldn't have gone at all. Granna's old,

Adam's little. Mom's had a heart attack. *Seriously, Mimi.* "Morning, my ass," I say. I pick up the gifts from overseas, step over the dirty laundry, and go out.

I let myself into Granna's quietly, in case everyone is sleeping. They are. Adam's face is flushed, one foot stuck out of the covers, one arm draped over the side of his cot; his animal book lies open on the floor. Granna is on the couch. She looks old. Her cheeks sag and quiver with each light snore that escapes her open mouth. I love her.

In the bedroom, Mom is awake. She looks at me and says, "You're back." Her eyes, under heavy, half-closed lids, look dull.

I'm glad to see you, too. "How are you feeling, Mom?" I ask instead, dutiful. It sounds trite, but nothing else comes to mind.

"How do you think? Shitty." The oxygen tank hisses like a whispered secret. Her hands stir on top of the blanket, the fingers dry as twigs, bent and misshapen by years of labor. "Just what I always wanted to be. A fucking invalid," she rasps.

"Do you need anything? A cup of tea?"

"Your grandmother is killing me with camomile. And kindness. Kindness, too, damn it."

"Maybe she has something else. I can go see." I don't move.

"No. I wouldn't mind a little TV, while the world sleeps. They show old programs at night, *Father Knows Best, Leave It to Beaver*." She looks up, focused on a point over my shoulder.

Granna has come up soundlessly behind me. "I wanted to bring up your TV, Eva, but I can't do it by myself."

"We'll get it in the morning." All at once, I can barely stand. "Can we share your couch, Granna, head to foot? I need to sleep."

The next day is Saturday, no day camp. Adam stays glued to my side, talking nonstop. After a while, I stop listening, just loving the constant current of his voice, the earnest telling, the energy that fills me and makes me glad. Together, we go down to Mom's apartment and bring up her TV and her magazines while Granna makes breakfast.

She hands me a plate with soft scrambled egg, a pancake cut in little pieces, apple sauce. "Give this to your mother, while I make more for us," she says.

"Sure." I take the plate. "I'll give you a hand in a minute."

She looks at me, steady and sad. "You have to help her."

"Help her?" I repeat stupidly.

"Feed her. She's weak, she can't do it herself. Put the extra pillow behind her back."

It's odd to see Mom's mouth open for each approaching forkful. Her jaw moves slowly, grinding from side to side as if checking for bones. When I look up, I find her watching me. I can't read her expression. Is it rueful or angry? Or both? I think I see regret flicker in the depths of her clouded eyes, a tremor of pain tremble across her cheek. *Damn it, Mom, why can't you just talk to me?*

She swallows the last bite, licks her lips, says something I can't hear.

"What?" I lean closer.

She grasps the napkin off the tray and blots her mouth with an uncertain, jerky motion, clears her throat. "Thank you," she says.

I never cry. At least I haven't in a long, long time. I leave the room so she won't see me lose it.

Granna takes the empty plate, says, "Good. Our food is almost ready. Five minutes. Here, bring her her tea."

I put the cup on her night table to cool. She looks composed; we both are. "I brought you an umbrella," I say. "From Paris. Look, it's collapsible, so you can keep it in your bag." I unsnap the tab, pull out a bit of the tightly furled cloth to show her the red-on-white fleur-de-lis design. "Very French."

"Huh," she grunts. "Don't know if I'll ever walk in the rain again. Or at all." She seems different, not so listless. Maybe the food has energized her.

"You will," I predict. "How long can you stand staying in bed? "

"Give me a sip," she says, her head turned toward the tea. "Yeah, we'll see." She lies back. I start to get up. "Wait." She raises one hand to hold me back. "Last night, after you all went to sleep, I started dreaming."

"What about?" I'm hungry now. I smell coffee brewing, pancakes, sausage. Her eyes hold me. I sit down.

"I was invited to a birthday dinner, me and six or seven other people. I don't know who they were, but we all knew each other, in the dream. Friends, I guess you could say." She motions for another sip of tea.

"Then something happened. I knew the dinner was over, but I couldn't remember anything about it. In the dream, I mean. Who sat where, what we ate or drank, what we talked about. Nothing. Like there was this void, this piece of lost time." I stir in the chair, impatient but also curious. I never remember dreams.

"For some reason, nobody would talk to me. They all walked around with closed, unfriendly faces, trying not to look at me. Some even turned their backs, like they were embarrassed, didn't want to be in the room with me. What had I done? Had I spilled the wine, dumped food in someone's lap, said something stupid? Had there been a scene, an argument? Why wouldn't anyone tell me? How bad could it be, and why couldn't I remember?"

"Mimi, come eat," Granna calls from the kitchen.

"Coming," I answer. "So?" Why is Mom telling me this, what

did it matter? We all know what happened, there's no need to talk about it now. Move on.

"So I woke up. I slept again after that, but no more dreams." She closes her eyes, as if all that talking tired her out.

"Forget it, Mom. You can make yourself crazy trying to figure out stuff like that. It's probably just your medication messing with your brain a little."

"Yeah." Her eyes stay closed, her lips barely move. "But still. They wouldn't talk to me."

Anna

Eva told me about her dream. What can I say? I don't know if I believe in dreams, not in a prophetic way. If we had advance information about our lives, there would be no point in living them. We need the hope, the surprise, the shock, to keep going. The problem to solve, like the crossword in the daily paper, that occupies the mind and keeps us moving forward, years on end.

There's something there, though, in dreams. Something about who we are, where we've been, what we're thinking about. Or trying not to think about. Eva's had a hard life; maybe she's taken more wrong turns than she had to, I don't know. But I can't help thinking that whatever we've done, or avoided doing, is the right thing, in a way I can't explain. Life doesn't have to mean anything. Sometimes it just is.

What turned my daughter from a sweet, trusting child into the morose middle-aged woman she is today? Foul-mouthed, too. Where did that come from? Ever since high school, she hasn't been one to talk to people, open up. Were there signs I missed, words I should have spoken, questions I failed to ask? Probably.

Now Eva dreams about strangers who shun her and won't tell her what she's done. She knows what she's done, and it no longer matters. Mimi is smart and reasonably happy. She's mostly fine, like we all are. If she tends to close up, like her mother, that's not because of any scars or grudges. Who doesn't have scars? And grudges are a waste of time.

It's a pity we have to get old before we figure out how to live without doing damage to others.

After breakfast, Mimi leaves to open the shop, taking Adam with her. She looks shaken, but I don't ask about it. I'm sure coming home to deal with her mother's weakened state is difficult for her. Myself, I'm beginning to see this illness as a gift, three women seeing each other more or less clearly, each of us defined by the pain in some new way. Maybe we're ready to welcome some peace into our lives.

"You're such an optimist," Leo said to me once. "A dreamer. You always think people are better than they are." Maybe.

I wash the dishes slowly. My hands look large, submerged in the warm water slippery with soap. It feels good. Washing dishes is so satisfying; a simple, essential task that restores order, makes things clean again.

I look in on Eva; she is asleep. *Good time for a nap*, I think. There is laundry to do, but it can wait. I don't feel up to it. I lower the blinds, lie down. Dream.

When I wake up, Eva is watching television. I hear the chimes and laughter of a quiz show: the question, the ticking clock, the hopeful answer. Ding. Time's up. Before me, on the coffee table, is the journal Mimi brought me from Paris. *Printemps. Les Jardins du Luxembourg*, a riot of spring flowers on the cover.

In the kitchen, I make myself a cup of good, strong coffee. I open the journal to the first page. The color is like the inside of the shell of a brown egg—not white, but not quite ivory, either. The faint lines for writing on are palest green. There it is, the thrill of starting a new notebook, the promise of a blank page. I think of all the others, deep in a desk drawer, each title underlined, the drafts numbered and dated. It's a life's work, serious but not important. I try to imagine someone choosing to sort it out. It might be better to just leave it alone.

I write about my dream. The memory of it fades with each recorded word, as if the motion of my pen across the page drains the experience out of me, leaving me cleansed, wrung out. I add no interpretation, no date.

Mimi and Adam come back in the evening. They bring fresh bread and fruit, make pasta for dinner. I start feeding Eva; she claws at my hand, takes the fork from me. She leans forward, trying to catch the strands before they slip off the shaking fork. "Damn it to hell," she says. The fork clatters onto the tray. She turns her head away from me.

"You're not ready," I say. "Just let us help you a little while longer."

"Go to hell." She is crying. "No, Ma. Wait. I'm sorry. I didn't mean it. It's just..." her mouth trembles like a baby's, big angry tears run down her cheeks.

"I know." I wipe her face with the palm of my hand. She lets me.

"I'm not hungry right now," she says in a nearly normal voice. "Maybe later."

Mimi and Adam wash up, put everything away. *What did you do today?* I want to ask. *How are things at the shop?* But it seems too much of an effort; I don't feel like talking.

After a while Mimi says, "I'll see you in the morning, Granna."

Adam says, "Bye." He seems shy. All this must be hard for him.

I hug them each in turn, kissing them on both cheeks, the French way.

I sit on the couch, not doing anything, not even thinking. I don't know how long. Eva rings her bell, once, twice. It's a small one, with a tinkle that sounds like crystal breaking, not at all obnoxious.

"Don't hate me, Ma." She looks sheepish. "I'm kinda hungry."

"What would you like? Eggs, oatmeal?"

"Too much trouble. You got yogurt? Yeah, that would be good." I've reached the doorway when she adds, "I guess I could use the bedpan, too."

I empty the yogurt into a cereal bowl, add a sliced banana, sprinkle in some granola, stir it up. The teaspoon looks small in my hand. I put it in the sink, take out a soup spoon. Better.

She barely looks at me when I come in, her head sunk deep in the pillow, eyes fixed on the television screen. I put the bowl down and slide the bedpan out from its shelf under the commode. "You know what?" I say. "I think we can do this. We didn't get this throne in here for nothing." I put the bedpan back.

There is fear in her eyes but she doesn't say anything, doesn't protest when I fold the covers back and help her swing her legs over the side of the bed. Together, we manage it—she leans forward, gripping the frame of the walker, the skin stretched tight over her knuckles; I hold her around the waist, help her turn, lift the edge of her nightgown, sit.

"God damn," she says, eyes closed. "God damn. You have no idea..."

Back in bed, she makes a heroic effort to find her mouth with the spoon, and succeeds, more or less, until exhaustion set in.

I hold the basin while she rinses her mouth. I straighten the sheets, plump her pillow, stroke her hair back from her face, turn off the light. "Sleep well, Eva," I say.

I walk around the rooms, touching things with my eyes. My things, familiar in every shape, every intimate contour. I turn no lamps on to dispel the dusk. Gradually, the crepuscular light dims, seeping out like a slowly receding wave, making room for the dark.

I stand at the kitchen window as if waiting for a signal, until the street lights come on. My hand passes across the smooth cool back of a chair, stops a moment at the corner of a cabinet, lingers.

In the living room, I sit down on the couch. I pick up my pillow, wrap my arms around it and press it to my chest. Outside it rains, hard. I think about closing the window but lack the will to get up. My heart beats against the pillow, loud, echoing the drumming rain.

The rain stops as suddenly as it began. I feel relieved. I don't have to close the window after all. There is nothing I have to do. Nothing. Still hugging the pillow, I lie down, my back to the room. I've always liked the dark.

Eva

She wants to be left alone. No, that's not it. Not so long as she has to lie there like a big old baby, unable to do anything for herself. Maybe leaving the hospital so soon had been a mistake. But hell, even with Medicaid kicking in it wasn't free. And who was going to pay for it? *Not like you're going back to work in a week or two,* she tells herself. "Fat chance, Cinderella," she says. "Your scrubbing days are over." So it'll be Social Security, with maybe some Disability thrown in. Period.

If only her mother would slow down a bit, relax. She doesn't have to be so, what was the word? *Sol...sol...come on, brain, think.* A fancy way of saying fussy. Solicitous, that's it. Okay, the bedpan thing is a pain in the ass. Eva snorts at the stupid joke, shifting the oxygen tube askew in one nostril. She pokes at it with her finger, gets it back in place. "See, there is something you can do. You're not a total lump."

She knows the helplessness won't last forever. If only it wasn't so damn infuriating. How long before she'd be up, back in her own place? Doing what, with all that time on her hands?

Eva turns toward the window. Afternoon, cloudy. Humid.

Anna pokes her head in. "Oh, you're awake. How—"

"The same, Ma. I feel the same, dammit. Wish you had an air conditioner in this room. Can't cost that much."

"It doesn't. I don't like that cold air, it makes my bones ache." She comes in and adjusts the fan setting. "There. Is that better? Drink some water."

"Don't want any water. Let me be."

"Okay, then, since you asked so nicely." Anna walks out. Eva sees, even through the drugged haze behind her eyes, the set of her mother's shoulders, the stiffness in the arms held straight at her sides. *Oh, shit*, she thinks. *I've gone too far. Again.*

"Ma?" she calls, not too loud, trying not to sound too demanding.

"Yes?" Anna's voice is crisp, controlled.

"I'm such a pain. You shoulda left me in the hospital."

Anna comes back in. "You were more of a pain there. At least here you have only us to boss around." She smiles. "Lift your head, I'll fix your pillow."

"Thanks. Turn on the TV, will you? And give me the remote. That should shut me up."

The police drama on TV was more than half over; she has no idea what it's about, and doesn't care. She likes hearing the voices, seeing street scenes, offices and rooms in people's homes, everyone so busy, so connected. Two men argue in a murky bar. The younger one fixes the other with a bold glance, says without raising his voice, "What you gonna do about it? Huh?"

The program continues, but she is no longer listening. The words echo in her ears. *...you...do...what...do...about...it... you...huh? Huh?*

Her mind shoots back to breakfast, the way her mouth opened automatically to receive another forkful of pancake from Mimi's hand. She had watched the hand, a little too wide for Mimi's slender wrist. Young, smooth, the nails short and unvarnished. Above that, her face, smooth in a different way, unreadable, with a slight tremor around the mouth.

It had felt strange to take food from her daughter's hand. Why should that be? Why should it be strange? People in families help each other. *I help her in the shop. I watch Adam*, Eva reminds herself. *Don't I?*

This was different. This, this feeding, felt humbling, like an admission of weakness, a dependence on the one person in her life Eva had never understood. And suddenly it matters, a lot.

She had jabbed at her mouth, her chin, with the napkin clutched in her own hand. *We could talk now, yes*, Eva remembers thinking. They would have found something to say, maybe not the right thing, maybe not the words that needed saying, but a beginning, a wedge that would start to crack the silence. If only Mimi had begun.

But Mimi hadn't begun. When Eva, in her confusion and fatigue, unsure what to do, had whispered "Thank you," Mimi had bent down to hear. So close, close enough to kiss, if a kiss had been what either of them wanted in that moment.

It wasn't. Eva had seen Mimi's jaw stiffen, her teeth clench. *You blew it, Eva*, she thought, watching her daughter hurry from the room. When Mimi came back with the tea, it was too late, the moment had passed, the thread was broken. All she could do then was tell her about her idiotic dream, about the dinner party, the silent friends. As if anybody cared what kind of crap crept into her head when she wasn't paying attention.

She pretends to sleep when Anna looks in on her, ignores her mother's sigh, hears the couch creak under her weight. Soon Anna is snoring softly. Eva finds the sound soothing; the natural rhythm of it lulls her into real, deep slumber.

She senses the presence before opening her eyes. Adam stands at her elbow, perfectly still, looking solemn in that way he has, the way he looks when he's thinking hard, puzzling something out.

She loves that look, recognizes in it the reflection of a child's mind at work. She knows, too, that it is inevitably followed by questions.

"Hi, Grandma Eva," he says, once sure she is awake. "Would you like a cookie? For after dinner, I mean. Mommy's cooking spaghetti. How is your heart tack? Did you have a good nap?"

Eva's lips stretch painfully over her dry mouth. She tries to smile. "Okay," she says. "Fine. Thanks for the cookie."

"I went swimming today, at the YMCA. We had to wear little pillows on our arms, so we wouldn't sink. Did you ever wear little pillows on your arms? I wanted the blue ones, but there were only orange ones left. So," he sighs. "You know. You can't be a crybaby about it. Right?"

"Right." She is relieved when Mimi calls to him from the kitchen.

"I have to help make the salad. See you!" Adam runs off, leaving a trace of energy in the room, the way some people leave a faint trail of scent wherever they go.

Mimi doesn't bring her her dinner. Anna does.

And then? More bad behavior, another unnecessary scene she regrets even while it is happening. She grabs at the fork, says rude things. Thinking about it, she cannot remember the words, only the frustration, a bitter ache deep in her throat, a sense of infuriating inadequacy. She remembers Anna's warm hand on her face, wiping away her tears, making her feel like a hysterical child. A crybaby. "Why can't I just die?" she mutters to her mother's retreating back. "That would solve everything." She stares unseeing at a nature program, something chasing, something running for its life. Eventually, she escapes into fitful sleep; there is nothing restful about it.

Later, when she rings her bell and Anna responds, her hair flattened on one side as if she's been lying on it, and Anna gives her yogurt which she, Eva, manages to eat by herself, she almost feels better. Using the commode instead of the bedpan is wonderful. "Doesn't take much to make me happy," she says to the TV after her mother leaves the room. She wants to say, *You look tired, Ma. I'm sorry to give you so much trouble*, but the words won't come. Because it in't about the illness. It is all of it, the years and years of her puny excuse for a life. "You're a coward, Eva," she says. "A fucking coward."

She dozes, vaguely aware of the TV, the drone of the evening news replaced by some mindless quiz show. Mimi and Adam have gone. Outside, the pale sky holds on to the last minutes of summer light. Eva hears her mother moving around, sees her pass from the kitchen to the living room, her stooped form framed briefly in the bedroom doorway. She looks old. "I'm sorry," Eva whispers. "Ma. Forgive me." She knows that saying it like that, to the wrong person, doesn't count, that you have to ask the one you harmed. That no matter how much you practice, it will never be easy. And anyway, Anna doesn't hear her.

She wakes to see a sheet of hard rain descend past the window, then abruptly stop. *Good*, she thinks. *It'll be cooler now*. The house is dark and silent. Eva wonders why her mother hasn't lit the little lamp by the front door. Maybe the bulb burned out. She turns away from the window and sleeps.

At dawn, she comes awake to the insistent demand of a full bladder. "Oh hell," she says, and rings her bell. There is no response, no sound but the cheeping of birds starting their day. In the street below, a motorcycle sputters and takes off into the distance, sending up fumes she can smell even at this height.

She rings again. Nothing.

She eyes the commode. There it is, two, three steps away, taunting her. She pushes the sheet aside, sits up. The room spins.

Put your foot on the floor, she remembers Joe's advice from so long ago, when they were young and drunk together, *to stop the dizziness*. She inches forward, feeling for the floor with her toes while reaching for the walker with a shaky hand.

The walker slides away. Eva lurches off the bed, lands on her side on the floor. She presses her face into the rug, feels its fibers rough up her cheek, her elbow; she squirms, sending a jolt of pain through her knee. "Fuck," she says. "Just what we all need." She raises her head and calls out, "Ma. Help me. Please."

Granna's funeral is quiet, just like her own gentle nature. That's fine with me. The last thing I want to do is talk about walking in that awful morning, after dropping Adam at day camp, to find her stiff and cold on the couch, a pillow clutched to her chest, my mother moaning on the floor in the next room.

A few people come. I recognize three women who had worked with her at the credit union and, since their collective retirement, attended show matinees and philharmonic concerts with her. Her lawyer, her doctor, her favorite bookseller also make brief appearances.

A small group I don't know stand apart, talking among themselves. I approach them. "How did you know my grandmother?"

"From the writing group, at the library," a man says. "She was so modest, always had a kind word." Tell me something I don't know. I remember to mumble "Thank you for coming," before walking away.

Who is that woman sitting with Adam, holding his hand? She looks familiar, in her gray dress and lace-up old lady shoes, doing all the talking while Adam, slumped in his chair, just nods and, finally, yawns.

"Who is that?" I ask Gunther. He seems to be at my side whenever I need him, which is pretty much all the time.

"Mrs. Rupert, from the second floor. She helped out with Adam sometimes."

"I guess I've only seen her in a house dress. Adam, what did she say to you?"

"She said I can come visit if I want. Do I have to, Mommy? Her house smells funny." He glances at the open casket. "Granna forgot to wear her sweater. She looks cold."

Granna left her condo to Mom, a trust fund for Adam. In a letter attached to her will, she instructed that I was to take anything I wanted before Mom took possession. In her letter, she says:

> *I was never attached to things. If I had a table, a lamp, a good winter coat, I didn't need to go looking for another one. You should all take what you like, and donate or sell the rest. It's only stuff. Don't let it stand in for what really matters, or raise resentments and bad feelings between you. Let it go. Be fair. Be kind. Love each other.*
>
> *As for the apartment, Eva, I know how difficult it will be for you to climb those stairs every day; it certainly was difficult for me, but I was used to it. Save your health, sell the condo. You'll get a good price, it's paid for. Enough, I think, to make the rest of your life secure and reasonably comfortable, if you're careful. And I know you are.*
>
> *Mimi, you got your share of my earthly wealth when you were in school, and when you went to France. Now it's Adam's turn. I wish I could have done more to clear a path for his future. I think you'll find the trust fund, though modest, to be secure. Leave it be, review it from time to time. It will grow. He's a smart boy, ingenious and imaginative. This small gift should help him get a start; his own initiative will do the rest.*

The rest was addressed to me, personally. I'm still not sure how I feel about her advice, or what I'm supposed to do if I accept it. *Oh, Granna. Why can't I sit down with you, drink coffee, ask you to explain?* It's as if I'm on my own for the first time, with nothing to guide me but her cryptic words:

Mimi, you are young and energetic and have good sense. In your business you reach past imitations for the genuine article. The cotton, the hemp, the silk. The real thing. You gauge their authenticity by eye, and texture, and experience. When it comes to people, it's not so simple.

Growing up, I never imagined I could make a happy life with a plumber, a man who cleared clogged messes out of stopped-up drains, who made sweet water flow where foul sludge had lodged before. It was no storybook romance; I don't believe in those any more than you do. But it was good, on final balance, and it was as honest as we could make it.

I heard someone say once, 'If you want more love, be more lovable.' It sounds like one of those trite sentiments you can buy on flowery drugstore plaques, but there's truth in it, too. Sometimes the real thing is not immediately apparent; even silk comes in many different weaves. Who knows what rich moments may pass us by when we are predisposed to disbelieve in their existence? I hope with all my heart that you will be happy.

I take Granna's antique desk and her notebooks. Also some photographs, her French coffee press, a few kitchen towels, and two cushions from her couch: red velvet, and yellow moiré.

"I want to be like her," I tell Gunther when it is over and everyone has gone home. Adam is asleep. Mom's fall left her bruised, her knee banged up but not broken. She is sedated for the night, with a home health aide on temporary duty. Gunther and I sit in my kitchen, a bottle of Cabernet between us. I cradle the yellow cushion on my lap.

"In what way?"

"The way she skipped the whole poodle-cut sweet little old

lady scene. The way she stayed real, like she says in her letter, refusing to conform to any conventional ideas of old age." My mind conjures the coffee cup on the side table next to her body on the couch, its stone cold contents strong and dark, unfinished.

He grimaces, half-smiling. "As if that would ever happen, you becoming conventional. Though, you know, poodle-cut sweet little old ladies can be genuine, too." He dips a finger in the wine and runs it around the edge of his glass.

"Don't play with me. You know what I mean." I watch his finger circle the rim of the glass, faster and faster, until the glass sings, the sound eerie and loud. "Stop that. You'll scare Adam."

"Adam? No. He'll just want to know how to do it, and what makes it work."

We drink our wine and laugh. It feels strange to do that, to laugh. Good, but strange, almost guilty. I stop. "No, really, Gunther. What'll I do about Mom?"

"How do you mean, exactly? Her care, or the other thing?" He opens the refrigerator, squats to scan its contents.

"Let's say her care, for now. I've been neglecting the shop, last couple of weeks. Customer loyalty only goes so far. Mom hates those home health aides, for some reason. But I can't run the business and take care of Adam and also care for her. I just can't."

His glance is not unsympathetic, but has a sharp glint in it. "Why are you still so mad at her? What's it get you?"

"It's not that!" The room is suddenly stifling. I get up and open the window, sit back down. "I can cook her dinner and stuff, and help her out, but I can't be there day and night, I have to—"

"It is that." He takes out a heel of sourdough bread, some other things I can't see. "Can't you see? None of it will work until you figure out what you want from her." He saws at the stale loaf like a surgeon or a jeweler, making thin, perfectly even slices fall away from the bread knife.

"What I want? What have I done?" I pluck at the edge of the cushion. "Okay, okay. What if I don't want anything? Just, you know..." I don't have the words. I'm tired, a little drunk.

"There you go. You've been shut down for so long, it feels normal to you. You can't imagine opening even a little to see anyone else's pain." Gunther warms the bread in the toaster, then cuts each slice into precise triangles. He stands at the counter, half-turned from me, an assortment of odds and ends from Granna's refrigerator spread out before him.

I stare into my glass. He's not wrong, but what the hell am I supposed to do? Turn myself out of my skin and try to be someone else, someone warm who knows how to, as Granna said, be more lovable? How do you do that? Where is this sweet water that will flow once the sludge is cleared away? Where will it come from? What if there isn't any, what if you did all that work for nothing, or only moved the clog farther out of reach?

"Eat," Gunther says. On the plate he offers, well, it is nothing short of magic, each piece a surprise. Fig jam and Feta crumbles with parsley. Garlic butter, cucumber, and dill. Rotisserie chicken slivers and roasted red pepper bits. Even that awful orange cheese Adam likes, transformed with mustard mayonnaise and pickled olive halves. The spaces between bloom with radish roses, carrot curls, and Granna's favorite tiny sweet cornichons.

"Holy shit," I say. "Gunther, you're amazing."

He shrugs, and pours more wine.

Adam

I forgot to tell about the day Grandma Eva moved back downstairs. That's too bad. Granna's apartment is really nice. You can see more sky from her windows, and birds in the trees. Mommy said it was too hard for Grandma Eva to use all those stairs, even after she stopped being sick, and anyway, "People like their own home, even if it's not the best."

"Yeah," I said. "I sleep lots of places, but my favorite is home with you."

She looked at me kinda funny but didn't say anything.

First we took out the things Grandma Eva didn't want to keep, like her old bed and her lumpy couch and other big stuff, right out on the street. It was Sunday, so Megan from Mommy's store came, which is good because Mommy and Gunther really needed some help.

My job was to hold doors open, and to carry small things that Mommy put in a basket, like food from Granna's kitchen. Cereal and coffee in a can and tea bags. I had to empty the basket then go back upstairs for Mommy to put more stuff in it. After we finished the kitchen, she put in some clothes, a nightgown and socks. She put a sweater on top, but not before I saw Grandma Eva's underwear in it. I guess everybody has some.

When I wasn't working, I went outside and sat on the old couch. Gunther came out and said, "What are you doing out here all by yourself?" He wasn't smiling.

"Nothing," I said. I wasn't sure if I did something wrong. I mean, people don't usually sit on their furniture in the street. Just then a big white truck came. It had red letters on the side that said *Sal-va-tion Army*.

Two men got out. One said, "Pull the ramp down. This shit looks heavy." The *ramp* looked shaky, like the plank on a pirate ship, except nobody fell in the ocean since it ended on the road. First the men took Grandma Eva's mattress, and then her bed. The first man had to walk up the ramp backwards into the truck, then they both came out again. I really wanted to do that, to walk up the ramp backwards into the truck and then maybe slide down. Even just once! They didn't look too friendly, though, so I didn't ask. I said, "Where are your soldiers?" 'Cause they were wearing jeans and t-shirts, like me, not any army uniforms or caps. I didn't see any guns, either.

"We're all God's soldiers, son," the second man said. "Even you—"

Gunther said, all quick-like, "You better go in, Adam. Your mom has more stuff for you to do." So I never found out. Maybe Mommy can tell me later.

At the door, I turned around and saw the men put the couch in the truck. And that was sad. The couch was ugly and lumpy but I missed it, a little. Then I remembered that Grandma Eva would have Granna's nice comfy one, so the Army can have the old one, since they need it. I guess.

Upstairs, there were only a few things left to move, but nobody was working because they were having a BIG TALK. I heard Grandma Eva say, "Who's coming to carry me down?" Everybody was quiet, then they all started interrupting, Mommy and Megan and Gunther talking at the same time. They said ambulance and fire department and stretcher and blankets and first aid and emergency. Mommy was mad at Gunther because he was supposed to call somebody and he forgot. Megan put down the telephone and said, "There's a big fire in the next town. All the firefighters will be there at least a couple more hours. And the EMTs are out on a call." I don't know what that means, but it must be bad because everybody looked unhappy.

Grandma Eva sat on a kitchen chair with her arms on top of her walker. She said, "Well. This is a fine kettle of fish. You're all good strong young people, but there's no way in hell I'm gonna trust you to schlep me down three flights in a blanket sling."

I got an idea. "You could slide down, if you had a ramp."

Everybody looked at me. Grandma Eva said, "Hah. That's the first smart thing I've heard all day. It might even work, if I had a ramp." She shook her head. "I'll just have to ride my ass all the way to the first floor."

Mommy said, "Mom—" Gunther said, "Eva—" Megan didn't say anything. Grandma Eva got up and started pushing her walker toward the door. "Come on," she said. "I don't intend to sleep on the floor tonight."

So this is what happened next: Grandma Eva sat down in the middle of the top step, between Gunther and Mommy. Megan carried the walker. Oh, and just before we closed Granna's door, Mommy gave me some notebooks to carry down. The one on top had flowers on the cover.

"All aboard," Grandma Eva said in a funny voice. She started moving down the steps, one by one, while Mommy and Gunther held her arms. She slid to the edge of one step, then sat on the next one. It took a long time, but she did it. She came all the way down the stairs from the third floor on her butt. I'm not allowed to say ass.

Megan ran down ahead of us to put new sheets on the bed. I stayed with the others. At first, I moved down step by step like Grandma Eva, still holding the notebooks. It was fun, but then it got boring and I just walked.

When they got to the bottom, Gunther helped Grandma Eva put on a new nightgown and get into bed. I ran back up the last few steps and hopped down, because, well, because it's fun, that's all. On the last hop, I dropped all the notebooks. They went all over the floor in the hall in front of Grandma Eva's door. The one on top, with the shiny flower cover, slipped away from the others and fell down open.

Mommy stuck her head out the door. "You okay, Cowboy? What's all that racket?"

"I'm fine." I picked up the notebooks. "Look, Mommy. Isn't this the present you brought Granna from *Pahree*? This one, with all the flowers on it?"

"That's the one," she said. "Come inside, close the door."

"There's writing in it," I showed her. "See?"

EVA

Eva doesn't know if she is glad to have missed her mother's funeral; being polite to people was not what she was best at. Taking that fall had been no vacation, either. The pain in her knee and hip wears her down, persistent as a toothache. Several times a day, without warning, her heart picks up speed and rattles against her ribs, like a jailbird falsely accused and seeking freedom. She sucks oxygen up through her nose, curses the fatigue in her bones, the fog in her head.

"You took the wrong one, Grim Reaper," she mumbles. "You shoulda walked right past that tired old woman on the couch, you shoulda let her sleep. Why didn't you fetch me? I was ready."

She's home in her own place now, with her knitting, her magazines, her dollar-store pictures on the walls, her dust in the corners. Her mother's presence is all around. The bed, the dresser, the kitchen table and chairs, had all been Anna's. And what had possessed her to take the bookcase? It is filled with books by authors she only vaguely recognizes—Tolstoy, Steinbeck, Woolf, Proust, Dumas—some of them in French. As if she'll ever read them. There's a whole shelf of poetry. *Really, Eva. Poetry. Who you trying to impress?*

At least the bottom shelf holds some cookbooks, her father's collection of photo books about France, a tattered world atlas, some art albums. She will look at those, sometimes. Nobody can watch TV all day.

She even took Anna's couch.

"Are you sure, Mom?" Mimi gave her that piercing look, the one that drilled into you, deflating certainty, questioning your judgment, undercutting any self-confidence you might have thought you had. "Are you sure? Why upset yourself? We could sell it, and buy you a new one."

"It's not contaminated. She was my mother." The words catch in her throat, but this time, she stands her ground. "It's a good piece of furniture, and mine's a piece of shit. I'll take it." Her mother had died on this couch, alone, while she, Eva, lay unaware on the bedroom floor, blubbering for help, unable to do even the smallest thing for herself. Who knows how things might have turned out if she had understood the silence, if she had been able to reach the phone.

She does not regret having Anna's things around her. Using them, touching them, makes her feel sad but less lonely, as if she's finally taken her place in this family's story.

Who was she kidding? Of course being home is better. She's learning to manage the pain in her hip; she can get up, move around, make herself a sandwich or a cup of tea. Gunther, of all people, insists she use the walker.

"I hate that fucking cage on wheels," she argues. "Makes me feel like a cripple."

"Oh, honey, I know. I know! It's only for a little while, until you get stronger. Didn't you say your heart pills make you dizzy? Well, then. Just use it, okay?" He looked so earnest, so beseeching.

She gave in, even promised. "All right. Okay."

He's an odd one, Gunther. Never in her wildest imaginings could she have seen someone like that as her personal caregiver. Not because he's queer. Who cares what people do in private? But he is so, well, so private. He's been Mimi's one true friend since seventh grade, a constant presence in their home and in their lives. And she knows next to nothing about him.

He takes photographs. He likes nice clothes. Sometimes he travels. He would lay his life down for Mimi. "Not just for me," she said once. "His friends. He loves his friends." The way Mimi said that, *loves* and *friends*, Eva knew this was something extraordinary, alien to her own understanding of those words.

And what were they to do, after Anna died and Mimi realized she couldn't do it all? The home health aides had been awful, impersonal, impatient. They scrubbed at Eva's skin as if it offended them, turned her roughly, pulling at the sheets and leaving her exhausted, ashamed of being sick and weak.

"Don't blame them," Mimi said. "They're so underpaid. They run from one sickbed to another all day long, then go home to their own families, who probably expect them to do the same for them for nothing. We'll find another way."

"Well." Gunther had put last year's *Travel and Leisure* down on the bed. "I don't have any training, but I've had plenty of practice. I am the master of sponge baths and funny stories."

"Wait—Gunther." Mimi looked at him. "You're saying you would..."

"Yes. I would. If Eva will have me." He gestured at the spread of Mallorca views on the open page. "Just look at these pictures. They're so banal. These hacks should turn in their cameras and go sell insurance or something." He tossed the magazine onto the stack at Eva's bedside. "So?"

He is wonderful. His hands are always warm. There is no shame.

Whether instinctively or through years of experience caring for gravely ill friends, Gunther knows how to wash one section at a time, exposing only her back or, briefly, her chest, one leg then the other. Everything quick and smooth, him talking all the while—stories of sightseeing in Denmark, dealing with incompetent clerks in the photo supply store, juicy political scuttlebutt. Eva is barely aware of his touch. In no time at all, she's seated in a chair, clean and dry in fresh clothing, watching him strip the bed.

"Have you been to the new Spanish place downtown, Silvia's? The best tapas this side of Madrid, I tell you." He snaps the sheet, tucks the corners as if he'd been doing it all his life.

"What the hell's a tapa? The only Spanish food I know is those tacos they sell by the hospital. Taste like dog food with spicy sauce." Eva's chin droops, her head suddenly too heavy to hold up.

"You mean that food truck? That's Tex-Mex, and you're right, it's awful. Tapas are nothing like that. I'll bring you some next time I go. There!" He pats the pillow. "Come and get comfy, and I'll do your pedicure."

Eva raises her head. "No. Not the feet."

Gunther stops midway to the bathroom, looks at her over his shoulder. "What? Why not? You too tired? You don't have to do a thing, and I promise I won't tickle."

"No. No. No." She shakes her head like a petulant two-year-old. "I can't explain. Just leave my feet alone."

"Okay, honey. Don't get mad." He pulls the covers up to her chest. "You rest now. Take your pill and rest."

"Who could be mad at you? I'm not mad. I feel all new, like a little fucking baby. Thanks."

He winks at her, beams his most disarming smile. "No bath tomorrow. I'll bring a movie. You like Jimmy Stewart? Great. I'll bring *Harvey*."

The nights are long. During the day, Mimi and Adam and Gunther come and go, or call, checking, helping. Afternoons, when Gunther has left and Mimi is still at the shop, Eva naps. But the nights are long, filled with dark thoughts and troublesome ghosts.

One night she lies on her back, watching the light from passing headlights slide into the room through the gap between the curtains, play across the wall, over the ceiling, fade away. She thinks about nothing. She thinks about her life.

It's a circle. Ma holds my hand on her right and Mimi's on her left. In the middle is Adam, looking up at each of us, his head and heart moving from one to the other, giving, taking. But the picture is fractured, the circle is broken. Eva sees her right hand hang by her side, Mimi's left just inches away, equally still, each with her fingers curled against her palm. "Open your hand," she says into the shadows. Who is she talking to? Mimi? Herself?

She sits up. There's a chill in the room, though not enough to turn on the heat. The silver radiator under the window is cold, she knows without touching it. She finds her robe, shrugs into it, awkwardly. She grasps the walker, moves barefoot into the living room, turns on the light. Carefully, heavily, she lowers her body into the gray chair, sits some minutes while her breathing evens out, her heartbeat slows.

Not knowing why, she reaches up to take a book, a thick one, from the bookshelf. The book is heavy in her lap. She strokes the pebbly leather-like cover, brown with a gilt filigreed design along the edges. She opens to the title page. Shakespeare. "Good choice, Eva," she smirks. "Right up your alley." Then, "What the hell." To spread the weight across her knees, she opens the book at random, more or less in the middle.

Eva slips on her reading glasses. *Coriolanus*, it says at the top of each page.

Cor. No more of this, it does offend my heart:

    Pray now, no more.

Com.   *Look, sir, your mother!*

Cor.   *O,*

   You have, I know, petition'd all the gods ...

"The fuck." She closes the book, lets it fall to the floor. "Who reads this stuff?" And why did it open there, why those words *mother* and *heart* and even *gods*? Was this some kind of crazy message, some *Twilight Zone* moment? "Am I nuts?"

She nudges the book with her foot, trying to angle it so she can pick it up. Bending over is hard, it makes her hip ache and her head spin. She catches sight of her toenails in the lamplight, long, yellow, brittle. Witch feet.

Eva hobbles into the bathroom, finds her nail clippers, sits down on the toilet lid. She pushes the walker aside and tries raising first one foot, then the other, but her knees won't bend. Stooping down makes her so lightheaded she almost falls off the seat. "Damn it all to hell." She flings the nail clippers into the corner under the sink.

Back in bed, she turns on the TV, watches Fred Astaire glide his stick of a body around the screen, doesn't crack a smile at his wiseass lines. She dozes off to the insistent predawn cheeping of early birds outside her window.

Almost immediately—or so it seems—the phone rings. Eva picks up the receiver, drops it, then lays it on the pillow next to her ear. "Mimi," she rasps.

"Hi, Mom. D'you sleep good?"

"Yeah." Eva clears her throat. "Yeah. Sure."

"You have enough milk for your cereal?"

"I guess. I don't know. I have yogurt. A banana. Don't..."

"I'll call Gunther, he can bring you some when he comes by. I've got lamb chops for dinner, okay? Call me if you need anything. Gotta go."

Eva closes her eyes, listens to the hum of the dial tone. Mimi's crisp voice echoes in her head. All business, all the time.

Gunther is such a mensch. I would never have asked him to help with Mom, except maybe for a little shopping. I could see him coming by now and then. Visiting. But every day, to bathe an old woman, make her lunch, sit with her? For nothing? Who would have believed it?

And they love it, both of them. The other day I dropped in to pick up some invoices I'd left behind the night before. Picture this: Mom and Gunther in the living room, reading, of all things, Dickens. Gunther doing the voices like a one-man show, Mom in her gray chair, laughing.

There's something I've almost never heard. Mom laughing. I mean, all out, from the gut, winding down to a rumbling chuckle.

"What are you reading, you two?"

"*Great Expectations*," they said in unison.

I actually shuddered. It was involuntary, like breathing. I'd hated *Great Expectations*, every godforsaken word of it. I knew I couldn't graduate without that English class grade, so I read it, gritting my teeth all the while through the ridiculous setup, the hokey characters, the plot milked for every last drop of melodrama. I mean really—clueless boy, haughty girl, secret benefactor, batshit old maid, good simple heart-of-gold man. I have gone to some trouble to avoid reading more Dickens; I just know that cast is bound to turn up again with new names. Don't get me started on the names! But I read that one, and damn if I can forget it. Thanks, Charlie, for invading my head forever.

Things were starting to look a bit unkempt at Mom's. I tried to keep it clean, but honestly, there's always something else I needed or wanted to do. She couldn't do it, and asking Gunther was beyond the realm of possibility.

"Hey, Mom," I said. "How about we hook you up with a cleaning service? It's starting to look a little dusty in here."

She stared at me. It was that cold, cold-eyed look I knew so well, the one that told you you were completely out of your mind to even think of what you'd just said, it was that stupid or crazy. "Look." I wasn't about to back down. "I can't do it all, and neither can you. I can pay for it until Granna's condo is sold. Then you can pick it up, if you want."

"You want to send me a fucking *maid*? For this hole in the wall?"

"Not a maid. A service. They'd come every couple of weeks, or once a month, if you'd rather. Keep things clean for you. I'll keep doing your laundry, and make dinner."

She turned on the TV.

"Mom, we'll still pick up and do the dishes every day. All you'd have to do is rinse your teacup. Please think about it, okay? I just want to make things nice for you."

"And what the hell am I supposed to do with all this time on my hands?" She kept her eyes fixed to the quiz show on the screen. "*Gone With the Wind*," she prompted the faltering contestant. "Everybody knows that."

"You won't be laid up forever. Soon you'll be going out, doing a little shopping, watching movies at the library. Right? You'll find plenty to do without having to worry about the floors."

She only grunted.

That was over a week ago. Since then we kept to the routine: the morning phone call, Gunther's lunchtime shift, dinner, dishes. I admit I've resisted taking the vacuum cleaner out of the closet, even when there's time for it, even when Adam could push it around as well as anyone. I was born stubborn, remember? It's my legacy.

The other night, we were just finishing dinner. It was Gunther's birthday. I'd pulled out all the stops. Seafood crepes, roast duck with apples, endive salad tossed with mustard vinaigrette. Mom and Adam put together a fruit and cheese plate instead of dessert. Gunther doesn't like cake.

"This is splendid, Mimi." Gunther poured the last of the wine into our glasses, topped off Mom's and Adam's grape juice. "I don't know what to say. Thank you."

"That's a first," Mom snorted. "He's speechless." She was smiling. We all laughed.

"I lived in Paris, you know, the city of perpetual delights. Bound to pick something up." I spread blue cheese on a pear wedge. "I should take you out for a cognac now."

Gunther and I locked eyes for a moment. I'm pretty sure Étienne passed between us, a flash, an image, a thought. Of course, Gunther knows nothing, really; they've never met. But he's my friend, he's prescient that way. He knows everything.

We shifted our gaze to Adam, watched him load his plate with fruit. It was momentary, but Mom caught it. "Go," she said. "Leave him here with me. If anything happens—and it won't—he can call Mrs. Rupert, upstairs."

"Can we watch *Rikki-Tikki-Tavi*, Grandma Eva? I just got it out from the library. It's about a mongoose." Adam wiped at the strawberry juice running down his chin. "That's not a bird," he added. "In case you didn't know."

"Sure, kid. Whatever. Use your napkin."

"Just leave everything, then. We'll clean up later." I kissed the top of Adam's head. "Don't wear your grandma out."

"Fat chance," I heard Mom say as Gunther shut the door.

"Gunther, why are you doing this? I mean, I'm grateful. Grateful as all hell. But I can't say I understand."

"Looking after Eva? Because..." he cupped the brandy snifter, swirled his cognac like a true connoisseur. "Oh, Mimi," he sighed. "Can't you see how damaged she is? Not just by the heart attack or the fall. That will heal well enough." He sipped, set the glass down without letting it out of his hand. "I've helped care for people, dear friends and sometimes strangers in far worse condition, dreadful pain. You know that. Eva's body is weak, but she'll mend. Still, pain is pain. The suffering is the same whether in body or spirit."

I was still buzzed from the dinner wine. The cognac might as well have gone right into my veins, its effect was so immediate. It felt good. I let my mind float, studied the bottle labels on the bar shelf. I downed another mouthful. My head swam and bobbed in a sea of Friday night voices, the pleasant din of people determined to have a good time, Gunther's words echoed as if from a great distance. *The suffering is the same.* I had never heard him talk like that.

Anger flashed hot and blinding, as if I'd been struck by lightning. "What are you saying? That I should be the one taking care of Mom, because her suffering is somehow my fault?" Furious tears burned my eyes. I ignored them, forced my words out one by one. "Just what the hell are you saying, Gunther?"

When he looked at me his eyes were clear and calm. "You asked why I do it. Maybe because of the way she nods and sighs when I rub lotion on her back, or the way she laughs when we read Dickens. Maybe I'm just selfish. Doing it makes me feel good. That's all I'm saying. Don't bite my head off if I recognize the pain, I've seen too much of it." He paused. "I just wish she'd let me do her feet. Those nails are looking wicked, they need trimming."

"I'm sorry. I'm such an idiot." I was suddenly tired. "I'm on eggshells around her all the time. Not eggshells, even, more like cracked glass, not knowing when it'll break and draw blood. I wish I knew what to do."

"Relax, Mimi. She's your mother. Cut her some slack." He drained his glass. "Want another?"

The second drink warmed my throat and chest. My head throbbed, but I didn't care. "Hey, it's your birthday. I almost forgot to give you your present." I pulled the packet wrapped in tissue paper out of my bag. "This just came in from Hawaii, for the summer vacation crowd. You could use a new shirt."

Gunther unwrapped the package and grinned like a kid. "It's perfect, Mimi. You always know what I like."

"Adam wanted to give you the one with frogs and iguanas on it, but I held out for hibiscus and what are these droopy flowers here?"

"Wisteria," he said. He draped the cloth over one hand and held it up to his chin.

"Yeah. This is totally your style."

"Thanks, doll, for everything."

We didn't bicker over the tab. He let me pay.

EVA

They're talking in the other room, trying to be quiet. Eva can't make out what they're saying, but from the sound of it, the urgency in their voices, she knows she has to find out. She can't just ignore them and go to sleep. So much has happened in the last couple of weeks, how could it not concern her? Her condition, her finances, her place in the family. *I'm the elder now*, she thinks. *Son of a bitch.* So she has to know.

"Gunther," she calls.

He appears at once. She likes that about him, the way he takes her seriously, makes her feel that what she wants is important. Whatever it is. "We thought you were asleep, Eva."

"Who can sleep with all that whispering? What's going on?" She pulls her feet in under the covers, but not before he has a chance to glance at them. "It's not still about my feet, is it?"

Mimi comes in and stands next to him at the side of the bed. "We found Granna's last journal. Adam says there's writing in it."

"So? Isn't that what people do with journals? Write in them?"

"Sure, Mom." Mimi rolls her eyes. "I just don't know if we should read it."

Eva looks at Gunther. His face is impassive, which probably meant that he disagreed with Mimi, but is too polite, right now, to say so. Maybe he thinks it's a family matter and he should stay out of it. She shifts her gaze to the window, watches a row of cars creep by, nose to tail, like a damn string of elephants in one of Adam's books. "She's dead, Mimi. My mother's dead." *As if you're the only one who cares. You and your Granna.*

"I know, Mom. But so soon..."

"Soon, late. What's the difference? Dead is dead."

"It's the last one, the one I brought her from Paris. She'd only had it a couple of days."

"What's the difference?" Eva repeats. "Bring it here."

Mimi doesn't move. Adam materializes by her side, his eyes shifting from face to face. "Go get the journal, Adam," his mother says.

"What's a journ..."

"Granna's notebook, with the flowers. Give it to Grandma Eva."

Eva sits up. "Adam, hand me my glasses." She opens the journal. "There's no date," she says. No one answers.

"'It's a big house, set back from the road,'" she begins. "'There's no...'" She lays the book down, takes off her glasses, wipes them on her sleeve. She pinches the bridge of her nose with the other hand. "You do it, Mimi," she says in a flat voice. "My fucking glasses fogged up."

Mimi perches on the side of the bed and takes up the journal. Adam drops to the floor, right next to Gunther, both of them cross-legged.

"I'll start over," Mimi says.

It's a big house, set back from the road. There's no drive-way; the only way to reach it is to take the footpath snaking between uneven rows of trees. The trees look immortal, impossibly tall, the blue-green foliage stippled with shifting patches of light. No sign of any fallen leaves, just rocks and moss and pale, nearly transparent grass. I recognize some of them— maple, beech, oak—but many more are unfamiliar. Some have leaves bigger than my hand, while others arch over the path, waving clumps of tiny silvery fronds like schools of little fishes among clusters of iridescent orange berries. I want to stop and examine them, feel the bark, crush the leaves with my fingers, but there is no time.

There are wildflowers, too. They twinkle, multicolored stars I can see in the forest depths, yellow, purple-black, red, pure white, the blue-gray of a summer dawn. I can marvel at them only from afar; I know I can't stop, or leave the path.

The wall of trees gives way on one side, my right. There's a steeply sloping bank that leads to the river. Here what trees there are look dead. Splayed, lifeless limbs attached to dessicated trunks angle precariously over the river. Naked filaments of leafless ivy stir like hair in a breeze I cannot feel.

"Is this about the park?" Adam says. "I never saw a river there." Gunther touches the boy's lips with his finger. "It's about a dream. You have to be quiet now."

Except for a band maybe six feet wide, at the shore where I stand, the river is frozen, even though the air is not cold. The ice is thin, charcoal gray with opaque white patches. It looks forbidding, but not dangerous; just still, stilled. By contrast, the not-yet-frozen part moves past my feet with silent, ominous energy, pushed or pulled by a force as irresistible as it is mysterious. To my left, a spot the size of a child's backyard pool shimmers with light, even though the sun hanging over the water is shrouded in mist. Blinded, I look away, waiting for the image burned into my eyelids to fade.

In the distance, a single small brown bird skims across the ice down the river's length, too far away for me to recognize. I watch until even the tiny speck it has become completely disappears.

The house is multi-storied, old, but in good repair. It had been painted blue, some time ago, judging by the weathered look of the exterior now. There's no particular style. Rooms and whole sections appear to have been added on from time to time, along with porches and balconies and even a widow's walk.

Through the woods, among the trees, I glimpse the roofs of other houses. They're not so far away, but I know that I can't get to any of them. The path I'm on ends here.

There are many windows. Some of the frames are painted black, like the borders on funeral notices. Others are primed in white; a few are bare wood, as if newly installed. I'm beginning to understand.

"I'm not," Eva sighs. "Where you going with all the fancy talk, Ma?" Mimi throws her mother a look, sharp as knives and just as serious. Adam yawns and rests his head in Gunther's lap.

The front door, painted red, looks too imposing. I walk around the long side porch. Through the screened windows I can see summer furniture, the chairs stacked together; my mother's sunflower cushions rest haphazardly on the chaise longue. I'm looking for another way in. I've always been a back-door person.

I enter through the mud room. There, among pots half-filled with dirt and the dried remnants of dead houseplants, I recognize the seed packets I had bought last spring—forget-me-nots, marigolds, portulaca, alyssum—and the new terracotta pots, the unopened bag of potting soil for the window garden I never got around to starting. There, too, are the radish seeds and green beans and peas I was going to have

Adam plant, just to see the wonder in his eyes when he watched them sprout and grow.

And there, behind the rakes and spades and hoe is Leo's hand mower, the blades rusted, bits of ancient crabgrass wound tightly around the wheel axle. He could fix it, wipe away the corrosion, oil the blades. Make it work again. I know he could.

The mud room opens into the kitchen. The first thing I notice is the fireplace. It's not ornamental, nor is it meant for romantic evenings sipping mulled cider. It's for cooking—a hearth. The iron hook has a pot hanging from it, etched gray with cobwebs.

Standing in the kitchen, I remember my grandfather coming in from the shed with an old corn popper, a perforated double-sided pan with long handles. We were excited to try it but disappointed with the results, the popcorn bitter with wood smoke, burnt on one side. At least I remember the telling of it, if not the event.

I see it now, leaning against the blackened bricks at the back of the fireplace, covered with the soot of who knows how many years.

I want to linger in this kitchen. Here are my mother's canisters, white porcelain with blue borders, Flour, Sugar, Coffee, Tea, lined up in descending size like Russian nesting dolls on display. On the wall, near the propane stove, a pair of cast iron skillets, a seasoned and dented omelet pan; on the back burner, a chipped yellow enameled tea kettle, the curve of its swan's-neck spout reaching into some recess of my mind where its impression has lain, stored, until just now.

Mimi stops reading. She reaches for the water pitcher on Eva's bedside table, fills the glass, drinks. Adam traces the geometric design on the rug with a lazy finger.

I must move on, obey the undeniable urgency that propels me from room to room. Each room has only one person in it. My grandmother in profile, holding something I can't see on her lap, some needlework, maybe, or a book. My grandfather's room is filled with leather-bound volumes and a variety of instruments—gauges and thermometers, a compass, a telescope. He stands, unmoving, at the window, his back to the door.

In a large room with tall windows, my mother plays a Chopin waltz on an upright piano, over and over without stopping. I pause in the doorway and listen for the mistake, a beat or two before the difficult trill that always tripped her up. There it is. I smile. She doesn't see me. No one does.

Then I hear Leo. He's humming that sprightly little tune from Bernstein's Candide. I open the door; he turns. My heart flutters in my chest, stops. For an instant, our eyes meet. Then his gaze clouds. He shakes his head 'no' and turns back to the atlas open on his desk, still humming and whistling to himself. Beyond the desk is another room. Through the open door I see my mahogany dresser, my favorite easy chair with the crocheted throw draped over the back, my journal—this one—on the coffee table in front of this very couch, next to a cup of steaming coffee. Myself on the couch, sleeping, dreaming this dream.

Here's one thing I marvel at with dreams: how memory moves seamlessly over time, shifting from here to there with no need of explanation, how you can be in both places and everything is fixed and perfectly logical.

"Daddy," Eva says. Her clenched teeth draw her mouth into a straight line. She swipes at tears with an angry fist. "Damn it. Damn it to hell."

Mimi touches her mother's arm. "Shall I stop? There's only a little more, but we can read it later."

"No. Finish it."

It's time to go. I find my way out, hurrying past other rooms. One has Eva's Nancy Drew books lined up on a shelf, a basket of knitting next to her gray chair. Mimi's room is adorned with Erté fashion prints on one wall, rock star posters on the other. There's a pile of ledgers on that little antique desk of mine, the one I know she's admired for a long time. A framed photograph of Gunther wearing a Hawaiian shirt, smiling. And here's Adam's, with Lucky the hamster spinning soundlessly in his wheel. Adam's desk has a scattering of French colored pencils, a drawing pad, thick books whose spines I can't read. On the wall, several blank laminated plaques, the kind that display diplomas and degrees.

These rooms are unoccupied, unfinished. Waiting.

I go out the front door onto the open porch. Off to one side is the duck pond. Yes, the same one I visit in the park. There's my bench, the apple tree, and, in the distance, near the filigreed bridge, the man with the tweed cap and his little dog. Nothing moves; even the ducks in the water are still. On the duck island, one stands with wings spread as if to fly. I wonder at this arrested moment, but not for long. At the far end of the porch, a wind chime is tinkling persistently, stirred by the breeze.

"That's no wind chime, Anna," I tell myself. "That's Eva's bell. Get up."

"That's all," Mimi says. She lays the journal on her lap, folds her hands over its open pages. "That's all there is."

Adam sits up. "It's about us, right? Don't cry, Gunther. Granna loved everybody. Right, Mommy?" He wipes Gunther's face with his hands, drying his fingers on his shirt front.

Mimi nods, her expression soft and sad.

"Us, yes," Gunther says. "She loved all of you so much, she even found a way to say goodbye to you. To us."

Adam

First grade is awesome. My teacher is a *man*. He has a beard, not fluffy white like Santa Claus, just a short one, kind of like the picture of President Lincoln on the poster by our blackboard. Sometimes he tells us knock-knock jokes, but mostly he makes us do our work, and no talking. It's not kindergarten, for sure, 'cause we eat lunch in the cafeteria and play games in the schoolyard. Then we go back to our classroom. We still get to sing lots of songs, though. My favorite is *The Bear Went Over the Mountain*. It sounds silly, to go see what's on the other side, but I would do it. You bet.

Grandma Eva is back in her own apartment now, but she threw away her furniture and took some of Granna's instead. She still has her old soft chair. It has some holes on the arms, big enough for my finger, and it's mouse-colored, with some spots on the back and seat, but she likes it. "It's the best," she says. It's kind of mixed-up, Granna's bed and dresser, and her table and lamp in Grandma Eva's house. I guess I'll get used to it.

I miss my Granna.

I had a panda shirt when I was little. It was my most favorite one, dark green with yellow bamboo growing on it for the panda to eat. I even cried when I couldn't wear it any more. Mommy got me new shirts with other animals, but it wasn't the same. I gave the panda shirt to Pete, my stuffed gorilla. He's big, but not as big as me. Now Pete wears the shirt, and that makes me happy. I wonder if that's how Grandma Eva feels about her chair.

Mommy only took Granna's old desk, the one named Louie. "Does my furniture have names?" I asked her.

"Sure," she said. So now I call my bed Roger, my desk is Steven, like my best friend in school, and my beanbag chair is Beany. When it's bedtime, Mommy just says, "Roger!" It makes me laugh.

When Grandma Eva came out from the hospital, she said, "No more work for me. I have to learn how to be a princess." She said another word, too, but I'm not supposed to repeat it. I don't know why it's so bad. It sounds like *trucking*. Oh, well.

"What do you mean?" I asked her. I didn't know you could become a princess, just like that.

"I mean I have a lot of time on my hands. I have to think of things to do. And I need help taking care of myself."

Well, I'm always thinking about things to do, and I can't take care of myself yet, either. But I'm not a princess! Grownups are funny.

So this is what we do now. When we get up, Mommy calls Grandma Eva on the telephone. Then she takes me to school and goes to work in her store. Gunther has lunch with Grandma Eva and helps her, but I think they mostly watch movies or read a book. After school, I stay with Mommy in the store, or sometimes we go shopping. Then we all have dinner together (except Gunther), and good night, see you tomorrow.

Oh, and Mommy has a new store helper. Her name is Megan and she's from *Australia*. I got excited when she told me. I asked her, "Can you tell me why a platypus is all furry, but it has a duck face and feet and makes eggs? I really want to know."

Megan smiled. She has big teeth and looks friendly. "I'm from Brisbane. It's a city, like Chicago or New York. I've never seen a platypus."

I said, "Oh. Too bad. You should go to the zoo."

She told me kangaroos can do boxing and that people like to watch them. In my animal book, it says kangaroos have strong feet with sharp claws that can cut you, so that didn't sound like fun to me, but I didn't say so. She's nice, maybe it would hurt her feelings.

I like the sticker Megan has on her car, too. It's a cartoon kangaroo with red boxing gloves on and she said she could get me one, if I want.

The other day, Mommy and I were driving home and she said, "How you doing, Cowboy?" We had finished talking about school and everything, like the poem I had to learn by heart before Thanksgiving.

So I said, "Um. Okay." I looked out the window at the people and the houses and the trees, then pow, I wanted to cry.

Mommy parked the car by the grocery store. She ran her fingers through my hair and said, "Hey." Then I *did* cry.

She put my head down on her lap and put her arm around my shoulder. She didn't say, "It's all right," the way Mrs. Rupert did at the funeral house. It's not all right. It's all wrong. Granna shouldn't be dead and Grandma Eva shouldn't be sick and who ever heard of a bed called Roger.

After a while I sat up and saw the wet spot I made on Mommy's skirt. "I'm sorry," I said. I tried to wipe it with some tissues.

"It'll dry," she said. "Blow your nose, and tell me how you feel."

I took a giant mad breath. "I know about how animals have to die, because some of them have to kill each other for food, and if they all kept on living there would be too many lions and snakes and everything. Is it the same for people?"

"It is," Mommy said in a quiet voice. I looked at her face and saw she was crying, too. "If people didn't die, there wouldn't be enough food for everybody, or room. We would get sick, and mean, and fight all the time. Wouldn't that be terrible?"

"Yeah." I sighed. I thought about the kangaroos and other animals that bite and scratch, or shoot poison into their prey. "But why couldn't Granna be like a giant tortoise? They live a really long time, quiet and gentle, they don't bother anybody and everybody likes them. Why couldn't she live a long time like that? Why does it have to be sad?"

Mommy wiped her eyes. "People are not tortoises. People have to be born and grow, go to school, learn songs and poems. We have to think, and work, and care for each other." She blew her nose, but not as loud as me. "When you think of Granna, try not to think only about the sad. Try to remember the love."

It takes a child's instinctive sensitivity to cut through all the bullshit: the words, the grudges and resentments, the anger whose cause is nothing but a vague memory, a ghost of times past. Like what's-his-name, Scrooge, confronting his own bad attitude. *Will I never be free of Dickens?*

I keep hearing Adam's words, *Granna loved everybody. Right?* How does he know so much? I don't know if I ever had that way of penetrating to the core of things, the way this kid does. If I did, I lost it along the way to becoming who I am now. Busy. Logical. Responsible. Derailed by the apparent importance of the details of my days.

Gunther comes into the shop around eleven, just to hang out. His rooftop photo shoot ended early, and it's not yet lunchtime. I'm putting up a shipment of new Italian buttons. I share some of my thoughts with him like I would anything else, a bag of chips or a handful of cherries.

"I'm pretty sure all kids do that," he says. "Even if they don't say it out loud. We're all born wise and clear-eyed. Before betrayal, before irony, we know everything important."

"Maybe. Though it's handling betrayal and facing irony that shapes us into the kind of people we are. Still, she did. Love everybody, I mean," I say, taking up the thread running through my head. "Adam does too, but his feelings are limited to this sphere, this damaged family, these people. Granna loved the world and everyone in it. I wonder if that was the secret of her contentment."

Gunther sits on the stool behind the counter, flipping through Women's Wear Daily. "And the heartbreak? The loss? Where does that fit in?"

"She talked about that, sometimes. Grandpa Leo died before I was born, when Mom was in high school. And Granna always talked about those years with my grandfather as if they were a gift. She was sad, but never bitter. Not that I knew, anyway."

A customer comes in, heads straight for the wool georgette displayed on the center table. "That just came in last week, from Spain," I tell her. "Beautiful colors." She buys the royal blue, reassured four yards will make a skirt and sleeveless caftan. "Send me a picture," I say. "I'd love to see how it turns out."

When she leaves, Gunther picks up as if nothing had happened. "And your mother? Was it a gift for her, you think, losing her father so young? How did Eva feel?"

I'm stunned. "I have no idea." And I don't. There was no father in my life. Why would I wonder how it felt to lose one? "We've never asked each other questions like that."

"Mm." He lays the paper down on the counter, turning it sideways to read the photo credits.

"Stop that!"

"What? I'm just checking out the competition." He looks puzzled, or at least gives a good imitation.

I drop the empty button box on the floor, stomp it flat before tossing it into the recycling carton by the door. "Stop disapproving. Like you won't say anything, but you think I'm a total fuck-up as a human being."

"I don't and you're not. I just don't get it sometimes, that's all." He puts the paper aside and strolls toward the door, straightening rolls of fabric along the way, smoothing the cloth down lightly into place. "You know I love you, Mimi. You couldn't chase me off with a stick."

"I know. But you haven't hiked in my shoes."

"Tight fit," he says. He glanced at my size nines with his sweet crooked half-smile. "Speaking of—it's time for Eva's lunch. I think I'll bribe her with pub fish and chips, if she'll finally let me trim her toenails."

"Good luck. You might need to throw in a beer."

When I get to Mom's, she's dozing in her gray chair, a new knitting project in her lap. For the first time since her illness, she's wearing a dress, the navy blue one printed with small white diamonds that she saves for special occasions. In the kitchen, under the potted geranium, there's a note from Gunther:

I tried and failed. Your turn.
PS—She got her beer anyway.

"All right," I say to the plant. "Enough of this." I make some noise putting dinner in the oven. When I come back to the living room, she's awake. "It's you," she says. "Where's Adam?"

I decide to ignore the tone. "Backyard camping with a friend. You're looking fine. What's up?"

"Gunther took me out for fish and chips. All that fried food, plus the beer, made me sleepy. Good, though."

"Nice. I bet it felt good to go out, right?"

"Damn right. But I didn't let Gunther have his way with me. No. He needs to let it go, already."

I don't answer her. In the bathroom, I find the cheap plastic basin they give patients in the hospital. I dump out the things that had accumulated in it since she's been home—samples of toothpaste and shampoo, mouthwash, a shower cap, eye drops. I fill it with warm water, swish in a squirt of liquid soap.

She is knitting, her feet tucked under the chair. "Mom," I say. "*You* need to let it go." I set the basin on the floor. "Put your feet in here."

"What? Why?" She looks frightened, but I'm not about to back down.

"You went out today. Did you wear shoes?"

She shakes her head. "Slippers," she admits. "It was okay. Nobody looks at old women."

"Yeah, well, what happens when it gets cold? You'll tear holes in your stockings with those nails. You put shoes on, you'll feel like a cripple after ten steps, it'll hurt so much. It might snow while you're out. Is Gunther going to carry you on his back?"

She puts the knitting needles down. "You don't understand."

I want to shake her. I want to scream, *What the hell is there to understand? Why are you so obstinate, so sunk in your own goddam misery, so afraid? What would it take for you to trust me a little?* I bite the words back and let the rage subside. We've been down this path too many times already; it leads to a wall.

I look at her sitting there, the knitting bunched in her hand. The loose skin of her neck quivers. She is small, shrunken, her shoulders slumped in defeat. "Help me, then," I say.

She is silent for a long moment, her eyes lowered, motionless except for her hands rubbing against each other in her lap. "My mother cut my nails, in the hospital. Her . . . her hands . . . my feet . . . and now . . . now. . . . ." She gives a deep shuddering sigh. "Oh, hell. It was so . . ." she looks at me, her eyes unreadable. " . . . so kind."

It's my turn to be silent. The anger rises again; I fight it down. *All or nothing*, I think. *All or nothing*. "You think Granna's the only one capable of kindness? Is that what you think? And now that she's gone..." I can't finish the sentence, not sure how to navigate whatever turbulent waters it might lead to. Neither of us is expert on the subject of kindness.

I reach under the chair, ease the slipper off one foot, then the other. She doesn't resist. Her feet look grotesque when I submerge them, the flaking skin crisscrossed like an old dry leaf, the yellowed nails, rimmed with black semicircles, starting to curve against her toes.

I cover the basin with a towel. "You soak for a bit. I have to check on dinner."

She leans her head back against the chair and closes her eyes.

In the kitchen, I stand gripping the edge of the table, I don't know how long. My mind swirls with, what? Not thoughts. Feelings, yes, feelings. The way I'd felt feeding her, the rage at her helplessness, the weakness I had never wanted to see or acknowledge. I like her salty tongue, her determination, the crazy world view bent by the stuff of her life, years of struggle I can't begin to fathom. If she is crusty, damn it, she has her reasons. How else to hide the vulnerable part, the soft center that life on the fringe has beaten up at least once too often? What do I know about it? I have my education, my precious little shop, my Parisian adventures, my pathetic misbegotten love affair. My perfectly wonderful little boy. What do I know?

Something sizzles in the oven. "Damn, the rice," I say, pulling it out just in time to avert complete disaster. Talk about crusty. I add some water, slide the covered baking dish back in the oven, turn off the gas.

It has grown dark. Mom's face is in shadow; I can't see if she's awake. I shield her eyes with my hand, turn on the lamp. She stirs, blinks. Sort of smiles.

I sit on the floor next to her chair. I towel off one foot and rest it on my thigh. Slowly, carefully, I start to trim away the accumulated growth.

Mom sighs. "Somebody once told me we don't get to do it over," she says.

"Who, Mom? Who told you that?" The hardened nails, now pliable, fall away easily into the murky water.

"It doesn't matter."

I wait.

"No. We don't," I finally agree, when there doesn't seem to be any more to her pronouncement. How strange this is, the way her words fill my head with my own regrets. Mistakes, bad calls, overlooked opportunities, last chances. What is she thinking of? I don't know. I don't want, or need to know.

I start on the other foot.

"We just have to keep going. Wherever." Her voice sounds thin, full of resignation I have never heard from her before.

"Yes, Mom. Yes, we do." I flush the water down the toilet, come back with clean socks for her.

Then I do want to know. Not everything. Only some small revelation, some glimmer into her past. Something. "How did you feel when your father died? You were, what, sixteen?"

"Fifteen," she says. She looks surprised, as if the question has caught her off guard. I slip the socks on her warm clean feet.

"Lost," she says, after a while. "My mother loved me, I knew that. But she had her own grief. I felt lost." She shoves her feet into her slippers, hard.

"Dinner's ready," I say, getting up. "Come."

We eat in silence, scraping up the browned bits of rice from the bottom of the dish. It's good.

When we finish, she sits back, pushes her plate away. "I'll be able to do my own nails soon. When this hip heals up."

"You will," I say. "Soon."

About The Author

Born in postwar Germany into a family of Russian refugees, Marina Antropow Cramer has been a waitress, fabric store manager, traveling saleswoman, telephone fundraiser, used book dealer, business owner, and bookseller. She holds a BA in English from Upsala College. Her work has appeared in *Blackbird*, *Istanbul Literary Review*, and *Wilderness House Literary Review*. She owned and operated The Cup and Chaucer Bookstore in Montclair, NJ, for sixteen years, then worked for Watchung Booksellers for the next twelve. She left bookselling in 2014 to focus on writing full-time, and now lives in New York's Hudson Valley. She is the author of *Roads: A Novel*, published by Chicago Review Press.

CPSIA information can be obtained
at www.ICGtesting.com
Printed in the USA
LVHW091221231020
669547LV00006BA/1279

9 781732 709799